TRAINS TO TREBLINKA

Into Treblinka by Henry Foster

TRAINS TO TREBLINKA

A Novel

Charles Causey

Foreword by
Rabbi Bonnie Koppell

Edited by
Vicki Zimmer

ELM HILL

A Division of
HarperCollins Christian Publishing

www.elmhillbooks.com

Trains to Treblinka
A Novel

Published in Nashville, Tennessee, by Elm Hill, an imprint of Thomas Nelson. Elm Hill and Thomas Nelson are registered trademarks of HarperCollins Christian Publishing, Inc.

Elm Hill titles may be purchased in bulk for educational, business, fund-raising, or sales promotional use. For information, please e-mail SpecialMarkets@ThomasNelson.com.

All Scripture quotations are taken from the King James Version. Public domain.

Cover Photo: Deportation of Jews to Treblinka, Siedlce railway station, August 22, 1942. Photo taken by Austrian Soldier Hubert Pfoch on his way to the front. Used with permission from the Documentation Center of Austrian Resistance (DÖW).

Library of Congress Cataloging-in-Publication Data

Library of Congress Control Number: 2019919439

ISBN 978-1-400330096 (Paperback)
ISBN 978-1-400330102 (Hardbound)
ISBN 978-1-400330119 (eBook)

Trains to Treblinka is hard to put down. The story presents a renewed interest in the emotional impact of the events of World War II... the protagonists are deftly portrayed...a profoundly memorable story about Treblinka."
—*Publishers Weekly* (BookLife Contest)

"Everything the Jews left behind had its value and its place.
Only the Jews themselves were regarded as worthless."
—Jankiel Wiernik, Holocaust survivor

"I stare directly ahead as I take off my clothes. I am afraid. By not looking at anyone I hope no one will see me. I hesitate before removing my
bra. I decide to leave my bra on. Just then a shot rings out. The charge is
ear-shattering. Some women begin to scream. Others weep. I quickly take
my bra off… A burden was lifted. The burden of individuality.
Of associations. Of identity. Of the recent past."
—Livia Bitton-Jackson, Holocaust survivor

"Camp was a proving ground of character. Some—slithered into a moral
swamp. Others—chiseled themselves a character of finest
crystal. We were cut with a sharp instrument. Its blade bit painfully
into our bodies, yet in our souls, it found fields to till.
We had all become just our bare essence. A man was seen and
valued for what he really was."
—Witold Pilecki, Holocaust survivor

for
Micaela and Olivia
may your lives shine through those who love you

CONTENTS

FOREWORD

Charles Causey has written a gripping, sobering account of the horrors of the Nazi regime at the Treblinka extermination camp. This is not an easy book to read, yet it is powerful and important.

Currently a chaplain in the U.S. military, Charles has served in the army for thirty years. As a graduate of the U.S. Army War College, where he was awarded a master of strategic studies degree, as a recipient of the Bronze Star medal, and as a student of history and the author of several books, Chaplain Causey is uniquely poised to tell this story with deep insights from a variety of perspectives. His writing is informed both by his military training as well as his insight into the human condition.

I met Chaplain Causey during my thirty-eight years of service as a chaplain in the U.S. Army Reserve. I had the honor of serving as the first female rabbi in the U.S. military, and Charles supported my work every step of the way. His professionalism and collegiality were, and are, legendary in the Chaplain Corps. In his various roles, he has gained unique insight into human behavior, which he brings to bear in drawing the characters in *Trains to Treblinka*.

The boldness of the human spirit, the depths of evil of which we are capable, the will to survive, and the ability to retain a sense of humanity when all around people are losing theirs—these themes come alive in his writing. Chaplain Causey does not shirk from describing the incredible depravity of the guards at the extermination camp. It is painful, gruesome—to read of the cruelty of those who killed for sport, including ripping infants from their mothers' loving arms. Yet we cannot ignore or deny history. Charles honors the memory of those who were lost by recording their story. He reminds us that our character is the sum of the choices we make, and that in every situation we have a choice as to how we respond.

Some of the Nazi victims succumbed to despair. Others plotted insurrection and escape, against impossible odds, demonstrating heroic courage in the face of tortuously inhuman conditions. Their story is captivating. Their perseverance and bravery are inspirations, and we owe a debt of gratitude to Charles Causey for giving voice to their story.

We live at a time when there are those who deny that the Holocaust occurred. As a rabbi and Jewish leader, I am profoundly grateful to Chaplain Causey for honoring the souls of the almost one million who perished at the Treblinka extermination camp.

Rabbi Bonnie Koppell
CH (COL) USAR, Retired
Phoenix, AZ

AUTHOR'S NOTE

The former death camp in Poland known as Treblinka is usually discussed in numbers instead of names. Like Auschwitz, Treblinka was a massive annihilation site during WWII. Unlike Auschwitz, Treblinka was not a slave labor camp where the Nazis took worker photographs and issued prisoners striped uniforms. Treblinka was strictly an extermination center. Its chief purpose was to eliminate new arrivals as quickly as possible. The SS leaders at Treblinka did not take time to mark the incoming masses with numbered tattoos or perform medical experiments. Instead they crafted an extremely efficient killing machine—their pinnacle effort. Few stories in history are as diabolical as the story of Treblinka.

The idea to write *Trains to Treblinka* advanced while researching my last Nazi Germany book *The Lion and the Lamb*. In traveling across Europe, working with Holocaust museums and examining original source material, I discovered an astonishing array of eyewitness testimony regarding Adolf Hitler's extermination centers. Thankfully Treblinka survivors bravely testified at the Dusseldorf trial against their SS captors in 1964–65, thus providing a rich treasure trove of accurate, firsthand historical accounts from which this story is drawn.

Subsequently, all of what you are about to read is a factual retelling from October 1942 to October 1943. Treblinka was a real place, with men, women, and children who experienced the events detailed in this book—real people, real words, real actions. Every person in *Trains to Treblinka* existed in history, their words are their own, and their experiences are written in chronological sequence. However, this book is a novel by definition because I have included some of their thoughts. My goal was to carefully piece together for the reader a historically precise tale of human survival and insurgency that must never be forgotten.

For me, it is often emotionally difficult to study the fierce details of the Holocaust, but I felt compelled to write *Trains to Treblinka* so readers of all ages can remember these egregious events. The fascinating people I chose to describe were predominantly young, between the ages of eighteen and twenty-two—and one fourteen-year-old—yet all held a central role in the uprising. They are inspiring. Their lives matter to history. Treblinka matters, though it is one of the least familiar concentration camps. We will never know exactly how many human lives were taken from us at Treblinka, but even one life was too many.

The characterizations in this book are my own.

Charles Causey
On the 75th anniversary of the Treblinka revolt

THE PEOPLE

The Nazi Guards

Franz Stangl	Camp *kommandant*
Kurt Franz	SS lieutenant and Stangl's deputy, known by prisoners as "the Doll"
Otto Horn	SS corporal in Camp 2
Kurt Kuttner	SS staff sergeant, also known as "Kiewe"
Willi Mentz	SS sergeant who runs the *Lazarette*
August Miete	SS sergeant, also known as the "Angel of Death"
Franz Suchomel	SS sergeant in Camp 1, in charge of processing the valuables

The Polish Jews

Edek	A fourteen-year-old accordion player from Warsaw
David Brat	An older gentleman from Warsaw
Julian Chorazycki	A doctor from Warsaw
Al Marceli Galewski	Camp elder, an engineer from Lodz
Tchechia Mandel	A young woman from Lemberg (Lwow)
Benjamin Rakowski	A farmer from Jedrzejow
Bronka Sukno	A young woman from Warsaw
Jankiel Wiernik	A carpenter from Warsaw
Samuel Willenberg	A nineteen-year-old from Czestochowa

The Czech Jews

Robert Altschul	A medical student from Prague
Zelo Bloch	A former lieutenant in the Czech Army
Hans Freund	A young businessman from Prague

Richard Glazar	A young man from Prague
Rudi Masarek	A former lieutenant in the Czech Army
Karel Unger	A young man from Prague
Camp 1	The processing area, also known as the lower camp
Camp 2	The extermination area, also known as the upper camp
Blue bands	Jewish workers at the unloading platform
Red bands	Jewish workers inside the disrobing barracks

PREFACE

Nineteen-year-old Tchechia watched Bronka grab her younger sister's right hand and squeeze it while whispering something pleasant to her. Tchechia could see that Bronka was traveling with her entire family—four younger siblings and her parents. Tchechia, however, traveled alone. She was pressed tightly against Bronka's family while riding on a resettlement train, and she could not help but hear everything that was spoken between them.

Tchechia was a Jewish refugee from Galicia, Poland. Months earlier she received word that her parents had been transported to Belzec, a Nazi concentration camp in German-occupied Poland. Tchechia had heard nothing from them since. Now she was traveling from Warsaw to *somewhere*, all alone except for her new friend Bronka, whom she met earlier on the crowded train.

Tchechia, who had reddish-blond hair, stood in stark contrast to Bronka, who possessed dark features. Tchechia's father explained to her that she would not be suspected as Jewish because of her Nordic looks; she would only be identified as Jewish because of the gold Star of David on her coat she once proudly wore each day to school.

Tchechia was doing nanny duties for two aunts in Warsaw when Nazi policies forced both families to move into the Jewish quarter with hundreds of thousands of others. She had evaded starvation in the ghetto and began to hear chatter about a resistance movement when the SS made an unexpected night raid and shuttled everyone in her building into these cattle cars.

"Bronka," said Tchechia quietly. She was not sure she said it loud enough for her to hear, but Bronka pivoted to glimpse at Tchechia through locks of bedraggled hair. She looked anxious. Tchechia was terrified herself but knew she could not give in to fear. She had to be strong now, for she was all alone. Eighteen-year-old Bronka stared at Tchechia with inquisitive brown eyes, wondering what the fair-haired girl needed. All around them was noise, from the train, people coughing and complaining, children crying…but Tchechia remained quiet. Bronka smiled at her.

It was all Tchechia had wanted.

The packed-beyond-capacity railcar contained little elbow room and nowhere to sit. There was neither food nor water during the entire trip and they had no idea how much longer the journey would last. Occasionally they would stop at a station where passengers bartered with the guards to purchase a small cup of water for outrageous sums. But Tchechia had no money to barter with, and she was not standing near a window.

At one stop an angry Lithuanian guard fired his rifle into their train car, killing a woman where she stood. Though a few children in the railcar screamed in terror—including Bronka's sisters—the guard laughed and joked with his comrades about it afterward. The woman's lifeless body convoyed alongside their feet for the rest of the journey.

During the next few hours Tchechia noticed that many of the toddlers had grown quiet. Some continued to rasp and breathe hard. All of the passengers' throats were so dry with thirst, it was impossible to think of anything else but water. More delays. Tchechia's train was forced to stop over and over again to wait for other trains.

Obviously our train did not have priority, Tchechia thought.

Finally, the train squealed its brakes and stopped for good. The captured voyagers peered through holes in the slats of the railcar. What they saw was a frightening sight: a monstrous unloading platform next to a small, square station house ornamented with a single rectangular sign informing the passengers where they were—TREBLINKA.

PART 1

VALUABLES

CHAPTER 1

"*Mach schnell!* Board the trains, no delay!" The SS guard shouted the same phrase over and over again while the Jewish prisoners obediently moved en masse onto the railcars. It was October 13, 1942, a brisk afternoon, with the leaves just altering into browns and reds. As the golden sphere of the sun began its descent behind the dark hills to the west, menacing Ukrainian guards in green uniforms prodded the crowd with an occasional jab from the butt of their rifles. The Nazis sought to transport the Jews from Theresienstadt Ghetto in Czechoslovakia to a resettlement farm to the east.

Six-foot-two and built well, Rudi Masarek, with blond hair and bright-blue eyes, tenderly grabbed the hand of his beautiful young bride Gisela. Just married, he promised her he would never leave her side. Rudi, the heir of an affluent family business, did not have to leave his home and travel to the Theresienstadt concentration camp, but he did it solely to be with Gisela. Rudi was only half-Jewish and had decidedly Scandinavian features. He could have been the poster boy for an Aryan youth, the kind of person the Germans loved, with a strong, determined face.

Delicate Gisela, on the other hand, possessed darker features. A true beauty in Rudi's eyes. Both her parents were Jews and she pleaded with Rudi to live his life without her. The societal rules in Czechoslovakia at the time inferred that men like Rudi could easily escape the German occupation under pretense of being a Gentile. Yet Rudi would not entertain the idea. He loved Gisela with all his heart and wanted nothing more than to spend every waking moment with her, even if it had to be at Theresienstadt. Once married, their fate together was sealed; under Nazi law, Rudi was now considered a full Jew.

Rudi had a hard time explaining to family and his best friends why he made the choice to go with his wife, and he often fumbled with words when trying. It was as if Gisela was part of him now and he had to be with her. Their fates were tied together, and he always wanted to be in her presence. Rudi knew he also did not have to wear the Star of David embroidered on his clothing, but beginning on their wedding day, he stitched it on his coat and told Gisela he would wear it until they could both take off their stars together.

"Hold my arm, Gisela," Rudi said kindly. They entered the railcar and realized there was no more room, but the guards kept pushing in more people behind them. Thankfully it was a passenger car with seats, unlike the stories they had heard of other Jewish transports using cattle cars with barbed wire and only wood floors on which to sit. However, all the seats were taken and people were standing in the aisles, holding onto poles or the wall. They began to press into others as more and more people were crammed inside by the guards.

Near to the Masareks were the Freunds, another young Czech family. The husband, Hans, held his small curly-haired boy, and his young wife. Though married and a father already, Hans's light-red hair and freckles gave him a boyish appearance. He could have passed as a fifteen-year-old. The two families were neighbors in the overly populated quarters of the work camp, and often chatted at the end of the day just before lights-out.

Before their incarceration, Rudi had served in the Czech Army as a lieutenant; Hans had worked in textiles with his father. Jews who had served in the military or had powerful connections were rounded up inside Germany, Austria, and Czechoslovakia at local train stations, then made the trek to the small work community in Theresienstadt.

"How long do you think we will have to stand here?" Gisela asked Rudi, trying not to sound too upset and become a burden.

"If they are taking us to a camp near Warsaw, then it shouldn't be more than one full day," answered Rudi. He could not imagine having to tell Gisela she must stand for two to three days, and he hoped that those sitting would exchange places with them after a few hours. "Perhaps by tomorrow's supper we will be there, having our first meal."

Gisela smiled at him, but Rudi could see in her eyes the dismay of having to leave their familiar surroundings.

★ ★ ★ ★ ★   ★ ★ ★ ★ ★

Hans spent the first couple of hours entertaining his son to keep him from crying. However, the original warmth from the mass of bodies that permeated the train dissipated with the early morning air surrounding the railcar. The boy's cheeks were cold, so his mother wrapped him inside her coat and held him close while Hans kept an arm around her.

Rudi and Gisela tried to rest. Rudi crouched down on one knee whereby Gisela could sit and lean her head into his broad chest. The monotonous metallic rhythm of the train served to lull most of the passengers to sleep. *We must be in Poland by now*, Rudi thought.

Through the window, the outline of the trees could be seen against the horizon; the break of dawn would come soon. Rudi dozed off and on, even with the unsupported, erect carriage of his muscular back swaying with the moving train. Each time he awoke he was reminded of the horror of the mass migration in which he and Gisela were forced to participate. He was angry. His military training as an officer taught him to lead and to resist aggression, but he could not see his way clear this time. There were always too many guards, and a tightly controlled environment. The slim odds of escaping with Gisela never gave him enough hope to consider a workable plan. They were being led, against their will, and he could not do a thing about it, except to stare at the early morning fog drifting through the passing fields.

★ ★ ★ ★ ★   ★ ★ ★ ★ ★

Clickety-clack. Along the rails the train continued throughout the night and rolled into its second and then third day of the journey. It was Thursday, October 15th. Everyone who was packed on the train was hungry, tired, and irritated; babies were crying, adults were shouting at their captors, the aged were offering prayers to the Almighty. Every so often the train had to stop at signals to allow other trains to pass through. When this happened some of the guards jumped down onto the platforms where passengers pleaded with them for water or for food. Occasionally, for money, a guard could be convinced to forfeit some drinking water for the privileged few who could pay him. The rest continued to suffer. Some of the Ukrainian guards began to taunt the passengers and make fun of them.

The Masareks and the Freunds were at wit's end. Due to their restricted movement, they were forced to urinate, and worse, to pass waste at their feet and the feet of those standing nearby—it brought them to new levels of embarrassment and indignity. As more travelers added to the mess the stench became horrific. One poor woman had dysentery and could not keep herself contained. Hans continued to coddle and woo his young child, giving his dear wife a break. No one could sit or kneel anymore because of the smelly matter on the floorboards. They leaned into each other, and occasionally toppled this way and that as the train lurched forward or came to a momentary stop.

People asked inquisitively of the guards if they were going to Ukraine or to Poland, and the guards simply laughed at the question. Most believed they had traveled a greater distance than Warsaw, so if they did not stop today then it suggested they would travel onward to Ukraine. Others did not care to speculate; they just wanted freedom from the train.

Rudi could tell that Gisela was suffering. Her face looked thinner and there was hunger in her eyes and mannerisms. Rudi looked at her small stomach and hoped to God they would arrive at their destination soon. He glanced at the Freunds, and sensed they were at their limit with the child between them. He slept restlessly, and sometimes whimpered. Hans frequently caressed the boy's smooth cheeks. *How much more could they endure?*

At last the brakes squealed. The train came to a stop then moved forward again. Part of the train behind detached while their car, and those attached to the front, began to move backward through a large gate. Another screech of the brakes and a whistle, then it became quiet for a moment. They noticed the scrub pine trees anchored into the sandy earth all around the train. There was a green fence near a little brick station, and an immense train platform. The sign out front said TREBLINKA. The train did not move again.

CHAPTER 2

Franz Stangl, *kommandant* of Treblinka, stood off to the side of the rail station and went unnoticed as the train from Theresienstadt pulled in to unload its contents. Neatly dressed with a pressed white jacket, deer leather gloves, riding pants, and shiny black boots, Stangl held a small riding crop and tapped it against the top of his boots. There was a smile on his face that morning. *This will be a good day for the workers*, he thought.

Stangl's leadership at Treblinka made him the immediate supervisor of twenty-four SS men, and approximately 120 Ukrainian guards used as an auxiliary police force. The Ukrainians were employed mostly for the guard towers and patrols, tasks the regular SS men did not want to do. Stangl had worked as *kommandant* of the Sobibor concentration camp for six months before coming to Treblinka to get things "cleaned up." The money and other valuables taken from the Jews at Treblinka had not been properly transferred back to the Nazi hierarchy by his predecessor, but that obstruction was immediately fixed when Stangl took over. He was a faithful lieutenant.

Austrian-born Franz Stangl was the son of a dragoon for the Austro-Hungarian Imperial Army. As a boy, Stangl used to look at his father's uniform with loathing; it seemed to him his father was more obsessed with his former military service than he was with the present, and with his family. Yet now Stangl stood in a uniform himself.

Stangl had been married for seven years. However, this current duty and his previous assignment at Sobibor took him away from his wife, who remained at Linz, in Upper Austria. He had developed a love for horses, which he rode often, even at Treblinka. Working at Treblinka was a top-secret mission. There were only a handful of men who were allowed to know what was happening there. Stangl reported directly to another Austrian, Odilo Globocnik, who everyone knew was a personal friend of Heinrich Himmler, the national leader of the SS and the Gestapo.

That morning, Stangl entertained himself by watching his workers assist with processing the new arrivals. Like dye diffusing into a glass of water, the passengers quickly spread across the massive train platform. A few SS men floated around to keep eyes on everything and maintain control. There were also twenty armed Ukrainian guards on the unloading platform, accompanied by forty to fifty Jewish workers wearing bluish armbands to assist with the new arrivals. Additionally, nurses and litter teams were on hand to aid the infirmed. A railcar opened directly in front of Stangl and, just as he presumed, the Jews who were disembarking were dressed well and carrying luggage.

The transports from the west were so very different than those from the east in terms of wealth. When Jews came in from France, Holland, Germany, or Czechoslovakia, there were vast amounts of food, clothing, and valuables that accompanied them. When Gypsies or Jews from rural Russia or Ukraine unloaded, they barely had anything besides the rags on their bodies. Stangl knew that his workers were happy to receive trains from the west because they would eat like kings for a few days, and the clothing would not be so infested with lice.

While supervising the well-oiled machine he had created, the *kommandant* reflected on the day he first arrived at Treblinka. *What a mess!*

He had performed admirably since then, Stangl thought: cleaned up Treblinka, limited the shootings, and sent all the valuables to headquarters where they belonged. His supervisor, Odilo Globocnik, was wise to choose him. "So dependable," Globocnik said of him. Stangl had ensured that all the valuables delivered to Treblinka were properly organized and re-shipped out to support the war effort. His predecessor had not been such a professional.

While the second and third cars continued to unload, scores of bedraggled people of all ages came pouring out. Wide-eyed youth, aged people assisted by Stangl's Jewish workers, and middle-aged couples often with young children or infants in their arms; everyone came out of the train wondering where they were, and what was going to happen to them next. A mass of people continued to pour over every inch of the platform. Guards began shouting. One used a whip to get their attention. Dead bodies were carried out of the railcars and placed onto wagons. It was chaotic, and after an hour of observation Stangl decided to turn his attention toward getting something to eat at the new bakery. A Jewish baker from Vienna made extra tasty pastries exclusively for the *kommandant*.

CHAPTER 3

When the train stopped at Treblinka, Tchechia noticed that the crude Lithuanian guards who had accompanied the transport to prevent escapes were no longer in sight. They had all exited the train before passing through the final gates of the camp. When the doors opened to the landing platform, the train's occupants were met by Ukrainian guards with whips and rifles.

"*Raus! Raus!* Get out! Quickly now, women to the right, men to the left."

What first struck Tchechia as she waited her turn to depart was the bright sunlight and influx of new air once the door had opened. Those near the door quickly lifted out the woman who had been shot along with another older gentleman who had died on the trip. This way the bodies would not be trampled upon when the passengers departed. The guards did not like the delay.

"Leave them alone! Get out at once! Step on those who are in the way!"

Tchechia stepped down and then looked back to watch Bronka's father shepherding his wife and little ones off the train. One by one he grabbed the younger children with his large hands thrust into their armpits and unloaded them to the platform. Then Bronka grabbed her two younger sisters' hands and moved in Tchechia's direction.

The guards stood by the railcar doors and used the butts of their rifles to smash people in their heads or backs if they were not moving fast enough. While it was invigorating to finally be free of the train, the physical torment and a new, odious smell of death had shocked and nauseated them. People tripped over each other and screamed at the chaos. Several shots were fired into the crowd at those who moved too slowly, or in the wrong direction. The numerous Jewish workers with blue armbands were also yelling instructions and trying to assist the armed guards. It served its purpose to heighten everyone's anxiety into a hysteria.

"Women to the right, men to the left! Women to the right, men to the left! Children are to stay with their mothers!"

Tchechia watched as Bronka's father hugged his wife and daughters, then grabbed his son's hand and disappeared into an ever-growing mass of men. More and more railcar doors were opened; hundreds upon hundreds of passengers continued to enter into the mass of people. The guards separated families and marched them out of the area. The women and children departed the platform and walked through a large gate covered with pine branches. They entered a courtyard with mounds of different types of clothing and were instructed to proceed into a nearby wooden building for processing.

Tchechia stayed close to Bronka, thinking, *If nothing else, perhaps I can help her take care of her sisters.*

Inside the building there were Jewish workers with red armbands and German SS guards who closely watched everyone entering the large warehouse. When Tchechia entered the building she saw women and children undressing, right there in front of the male guards. More yelling. More instructions. Women were told to remove all clothing and place it into piles: shoes in one place, dresses in another, underwear over there, and coats by the door. Up ahead, already undressed women were forced into another room where a guard yelled something about haircuts for delousing. They were headed for the showers, but for some reason were told to keep their valuables, jewelry, and identification papers with them.

While Tchechia began to undress, a nasty-looking SS guard with drool at one corner of his mouth walked up to her holding a whip.

"What is your name?"

"Tchechia."

"Where are you from?"

"Lemberg."

"You do not look Jewish," the guard said matter-of-factly.

Tchechia did not respond. She continued to undress while keeping eye contact with Bronka. Once naked, Tchechia grabbed all her clothing and scurried over to the piles where she deposited her belongings into the designated spaces. Then she moved over to the line where the women were waiting to have their hair cut.

Just before Tchechia entered the shearing room, a Jewish worker with a red band on his sleeve tapped her on the shoulder.

"You there, come over here," he said.

"Why?" asked Tchechia. She grew suspicious, and wondered why she was not allowed to have her hair cut and proceed to the showers.

"Because we need you for work, that's why. Now quit asking questions and find some clothes to put on. You will be thankful later."

The camp worker turned and made eye contact with the SS guard who had first spoken to Tchechia. He was standing there smiling, approvingly. She saw their silent exchange, then quickly moved back to the piles to search for her clothes.

Tchechia looked around and noticed that, among the masses of women and children, there were several other young girls getting dressed again. She looked for Bronka and saw her speaking to a different SS guard. He was explaining something to her. Bronka was pointing to her mother and sisters who were heading into the shearing room, and it appeared Bronka was pleading with the guard to stay with her family. He kept shaking his head and telling her something. Tchechia quickly dressed and ran over to Bronka.

"Bronka, what did he say to you?" asked Tchechia.

"He asked if I was a seamstress and I told him no. He then told me I *was certainly* a seamstress, and that they needed me to work here at the camp." Bronka had tears streaming down her face.

"Don't cry, Bronka! We can get our showers later."

"They've taken all of my family away from me, Tchechia. What if they are not going to the showers? What if they are taking them somewhere else and I will not see them again?"

While Bronka had been negotiating with the guard, her mother and sisters were forced into the shearing room and then disappeared. Bronka did not get to say goodbye.

"You two there, come with me!" A Jewish worker was rounding up the women who were told to redress. Bronka quickly slipped on a dress that was too big for her, ran to the pile of shoes to grab the first pair she laid eyes on, then followed Tchechia and the man out of the building.

★ ★ ★ ★ ★   ★ ★ ★ ★ ★

Tchechia and Bronka were led outside the large building to the courtyard where clothing and other goods were left in large mounds. Tchechia noticed the ground was barely visible in the courtyard due to all the valuables of those who had gone through the back door of the barracks. Besides the innumerable items of clothing, she saw watches, pens, hairbrushes, wallets, and even candy placed in enormous mounds so the Jewish workers could package it all into bundles for shipping back to Germany.

While the girls worked at organizing the items in the courtyard, there was nothing Tchechia could say to get Bronka to stop her weeping. Finally, one of the Jewish workers who carried a whip and appeared to be a supervisor came over and grabbed Bronka tightly by the throat.

"Stop crying!" he shouted. "If you don't stop, you will follow your family into the tube."

He released his grip from her neck and moved off in the direction of the train platform. Bronka ferociously tried to catch her breath. As they went back to work, Tchechia noticed the harsh treatment had seemed to knock the grief out of Bronka. Now she appeared more angry than sad.

When they stopped for a short break, Bronka asked Tchechia, "Isn't the man who grabbed me a Jew? Then why does he treat one of his own so unkindly? And why does he carry a whip? What kind of place have we come to?"

"I don't know," responded Tchechia. "But the important thing now is to play by their rules and do everything they tell us to do."

"And look at all of this stuff," Bronka continued as if not hearing Tchechia. "We have worked here for an hour and have not put a dent in the piles. This will take years to sort."

The two young women went back to work, not understanding what exactly they were supposed to do, or why they were doing it. They had not been shown where they would sleep, and they had not been given any food or water. They were simply told to keep working.

CHAPTER 4

Out of the train window, Rudi Masarek could see a flood of people already on the arrival platform. There were guards shouting and medical people hustling around, but the principal scene Rudi noticed were the bodies—apparently those who had died on the trip—just scattered on the ground with no one attending them.

Beyond the elongated platform were wooden barracks, and beyond them were fences with barbed wire that appeared to be camouflaged with pine branches. Now with everyone in the railcar standing and excited to depart, mercifully the door was unlocked and opened. Rudi grabbed Gisela's hand. They had made it. The next phase of the adventure was about to begin. *Perhaps it won't be as grim as Theresienstadt, where they labored many hours a day and were crammed into tight living quarters at night.*

The first instructions were shouted by guards peering into their opened door, "*Raus!* Get out! Everyone out! *Aber schnell!* Keep your hand luggage. Leave trunks and large bags in place. You will fetch them later. Quickly, you must move quickly!"

Passengers poured out of the car. Rudi and Gisela shuffled toward the doorway until it was their time to step down. Rudi glanced back and saw Hans Freund holding his son and helping his wife shuffle to the door.

"Mommy, I'm cold," Hans's son cried out.

"I hope he won't catch a cold," said Hans to his wife as they prepared to leave the railcar.

The young Masarek couple stepped down out of the train. They each held a small bag of personal belongings. The platform was long and wide. *There are perhaps twenty-five cars unloading right now*, Rudi speculated.

Several of the guards continued to yell the same instructions to those still departing the railcars. Then one of the guards uttered words that iced Rudi where he stood.

"Men to the left, women to the right!" the guard shouted.

"Rudi!" Gisela screamed as she flung herself at him.

Rudi wrapped his strong arms around his fragile bride. "I know Gisela, I know! But I don't know what to do."

"Men to the left, women to the right! Children are to stay with their mothers!"

The scream from the guard was louder now and sounded as if he was walking toward them.

"We have to part for now! I love you, Gisela, and I promise to come find you as soon as I am able. Think of Austria. Think of your grandfather's farm." Rudi quickly kissed her ear, neck, and cheek as the guard grabbed tearful Gisela away from him.

"I love you, Rudi!" Gisela shrieked.

"I love you, Gisela!"

Nearby, Hans said goodbye to his wife and curly-haired boy. He stroked his soft cheeks and kissed the lad and mother all over, just before they were torn apart by a Jewish worker.

"Goodbye for now," Hans said. "I will be with you soon."

Rudi surmised the situation, wondering if there was a possibility of escape. There were watchful eyes everywhere, and there were Jewish helpers with blue bands on their arms who seemed complicit with what the Nazi guards were shouting. *Why do they help our enemy? Why do they separate families like this?*

Children were crying, the elderly were being carried off to what looked like a hospital area, and men and women tried to follow the directions of their captors while pleading for something to drink. Rudi watched Gisela as she moved with a mass of women away from the platform and toward a large wooden barracks. There were thousands of men left standing on the platform. Gisela glanced back at Rudi, who could clearly see the fear she carried. Then she was lost from view.

Hans also stood nearby, watching his family depart with the others. His son waved to him and Hans waved back. Then they were gone.

Suddenly a guard shouted, "Undress! Undress! Take off your shoes and tie them together! Place your clothes on this pile over here. Wait in line over there. Hurry, hurry! You must disrobe and prepare for delousing! Take along your money, documents, jewelry, and watches. Hurry, don't delay."

Rudi and Hans undressed along with the other men and stood in line. There were SS sergeants scanning the crowd and occasionally picking out men and sending them away from the line.

When one of them noticed blond-haired and blue-eyed Rudi, and tall Hans, each with a well-built and healthy exterior, the guard shouted to them, "You two, you don't belong in this line. Walk over there and get dressed again. I will deal with you in a moment."

Rudi and Hans did not know if this was a good thing to happen or not, but it gave them the sense that something fishy was going on. They walked over to the sizable pile where they had undressed and tried to find their own clothes. There were twenty to thirty chosen men who were told to redress themselves. The rest of the men in the large group were forced to pick up armfuls of clothing from the mountain of clothing items deposited from the passengers, then ran naked with them down to the wooden barracks where the women were sent.

Once dressed, Rudi tapped the shoulder of one of the Jewish workers holding a whip.

"Excuse me, sir, but where will the women and children end up after they are processed?"

"They're going to the showers for delousing," replied the surprised worker. "Don't worry about them. They will be all right. In fact, they are going to have it better than you."

What is that supposed to mean? Rudi wondered. The Jewish man's face was not convincing. Perhaps it was because he did not look Rudi in the eye when he made his statements.

"Here's a warning: don't ever touch a *kapo* again if you know what's good for you. You're from the west and I will give you a pass this once. We *kapos* have a job to do and we don't mind doing it well, so stay clear of us from now on unless you want a beating."

Rudi soon found out there were a handful of Jewish men serving as *kapos*—also known as *collaborators*—who essentially worked for the Nazis and would beat their fellow Jews as viciously as one of the German guards. Rudi had heard about that sort of abuse taking place in the Warsaw ghetto but had never experienced it in Theresienstadt.

The SS sergeant who picked Rudi and Hans out of the line came back to the men and gave them instructions.

"All right," he said with a sort of distasteful grin. "You here who have been chosen today…my name is Sergeant Miete, and you will do as I say without question. First off, nobody walks here at Treblinka. Whenever you move about, unless you are in your bunk or at a worktable, you will move at a run. Second, if for any reason you do not immediately obey what we say you will end up in the *Lazarette*; your *kapos* will explain what that means to you. Now, help your fellow Treblinka workers unload all the trunks and suitcases off the train. If you find dead bodies in the railcars, load them onto the lorries. Then you will bring every item on this platform down to the wooden warehouse to be sorted through. You will not stop until this entire area is clean, understand? And don't eat the food; it is to be sorted and stored like everything else. In fact, don't steal anything or you will be taken to the *Lazarette*. Move out!"

The group of men ran as fast as they could to the train and jumped into the railcars to empty the luggage. Then they grabbed armfuls of clothing and hauled them down into a large courtyard near the wooden barracks where the women and children had been taken. Rudi and Hans hoped to see their wives in the barracks, but when the door opened and they peeked inside it looked empty, apart from some Jewish workers sweeping and sorting. *Where had everyone been taken?*

In the middle of the courtyard there were such large piles of separated goods from the passengers that it was staggering. There was one pile nearly fifteen feet high with thousands of pairs of shoes in it. There was another mound, even wider and taller, where people had hurled their clothes and belongings to the top. This small mountain took up a huge swath of the courtyard. Surely the clothes must have come from several trainloads of passengers, thought Rudi, and could not have formed only from the group who unloaded today. Seeing the mound took his breath away, realizing the number of people it represented.

Next to the mountain of clothing were bundles of different apparel, sorted and strung together in cubes, then crudely stacked into a pyramid shape. Men's coats in one bundle, women's dresses in another. *What kind of factory is this?* Rudi wondered.

The new workers were next ordered into the large wooden structure where their families had disrobed. They had to bring the discarded clothing—which filled the room—back outside into the courtyard. There were still a few Jewish workers inside cleaning the area, and each of them had a red armband on their sleeve.

The two men from Prague found out that the red armbands designated those Jews who worked in the wooden sorting barracks. They assisted with the new arrivals to help them undress and store their clothing properly. The Jewish workers with blue bands only helped at the loading platform.

Hans approached one of the workers and asked, "Please, sir, my wife and small boy were taken to this building a few hours ago. Can you tell me where they are now?"

The worker looked at Hans, then glanced around the work site to ensure they were not attracting the attention of any of the guards or *kapos*. The man said to Hans, "Don't you see what's happening here? These are all the clothes of the passengers. You shouldn't ask this question; it is the secret of Treblinka," he whispered. The man was very hesitant and deliberate with his words.

Rudi stood near to Hans and asked the next question, saying, "But the *kapo* told me they would have it better than us. What did he mean by that?"

"In a way, yes, but he was lying, as the *kapos* like to do. Just be thankful you were picked out and helping us today. And never trust a *kapo*!"

The men realized they had attracted the attention of one of the guards, who was headed their way, so they quickly disbanded and hurried to grab armfuls of clothing in order to run with them outside, but they were too late.

"Hey, you there," called a guard with an SS field cap pulled tightly down over his entire forehead. "What is that you were talking about and not working? Tell me!"

Hans matter-of-factly confessed, "I asked him where my wife and son are. Will you tell me?"

It was the way he said it, Hans and Rudi knew instantly, that the guard took it as a sign of boldness and disrespect. He lifted his whip and let it fling across the tender spot between Hans's neck and shoulder. Then, as suddenly as he was angered, his entire expression changed and he smiled.

"Now, now, don't worry about those tender little lambs you brought with you. They are fine. Your wife is working in the laundry in Camp 2.

Your son is playing with the other tots who arrived. Go back to work. Work will make you happy."

The guard made an abrupt about-face then walked away, mumbling to himself, "Work will make you happy, work will make everyone happy."

Their thoughts now scattered, Hans and Rudi attempted to work without anyone noticing how deeply disturbed they were by what had happened to them so far at Treblinka. They struggled to reason out what they had been told and what they were forced to do, but there was so much they did not understand.

They knew that at least two or three thousand people must have departed the train with them that day, yet they could not deduce where they had disappeared. In the large wooden sorting room where the women and children had gone, there were some barbers with red armbands who were taking suitcases of hair out into the courtyard. Hans thought of his son's curly hair and soft cheeks and almost wept, but they had to keep moving.

They had been working tirelessly when finally one of the guards mentioned food. The two men waited in a long line with dozens of other Jewish workers. Holding a dirty bowl handed to them by another laborer, they were given some soup and bread, then were again forced to sort clothing and make more bundles.

All around the courtyard, men in street clothes were running this way and that with large bundles of clothing on their backs. Their eternal first day seemed like a nightmare.

At long last the foreman ceased the work and they were taken to a sleeping barracks. The new workers had to quickly find a place to sleep in because the doors were being locked and soon it would be lights-out. It was here they began to meet other men from Prague. One of the men asked Rudi, "Hey, you there, tall Bohemian, you look more Nordic than Jewish. What are you doing here?"

Rudi fumbled with his words, something about Theresienstadt and being only a partial Jew. He and Hans soon learned that three of the other men were from Prague and they stuck together: Richard Glazar, Karel Unger, and Robert Altschul. They invited Rudi and Hans to bunk near to them and a friendship began to form.

These three other Czechs were also transported from Theresienstadt, also young and strong and tall, also numbed by the events transpiring around them. Richard and Karel were only twenty-one years old; Robert was twenty-seven and a medical student, selected to work in the camp pharmacy with the doctor.

After introductions, Hans explained that he had come with his wife and son and could not get a direct answer out of anyone about where they had been taken. Rudi, feeling forlorn and fatigued, stayed silent.

Robert, with a deep and compassionate voice, solemnly explained, "Men, if you had family members who went through the processing building and had their hair cut without a guard calling them out for work like you were…I'm sorry, but they are lost."

"What do you mean *lost?*" Hans asked indignantly. "I am tired of all these expressions people use. Lost? Please tell me directly, do they shoot them all?" There was panic in Hans's words and his eyes.

"No, they do not shoot them. None of us have been there. We do not know exactly what happens on the other side of the sandy embankment."

Richard and Karel glanced at each other with knowing looks. On the day Karel arrived, his parents and his younger brother were forced into the tube. Karel was still trying to reconcile the event to make sense out of it. Richard had come alone, but he doubted the rest of his family was still alive, *wherever they were.*

Robert placed his hand on Hans's shoulder. "Others have told us that there are large gassing chambers at the end of the walkway that we call the tube. So when the people from the trains think they are receiving showers, they are actually gassed."

This was too much for Hans to comprehend. It had confirmed all of his suspicions about the secret of Treblinka. He brought a fist up to his face and bit his knuckles. He pictured his young son with his soft cheeks, and his precious wife whom he promised to protect.

Rudi silently sat down on the bunk and pictured Gisela in his mind. He was awash with pain as he thought about the fact that his young wife was expecting their first child. He surmised she had died perhaps just moments after their sad goodbye. Rudi bent over, holding his stomach and swaying a little bit. His head was down so the others could not see his face. The lights turned out, and the male barracks building was locked for the night. Their first day at Treblinka had come to an end.

CHAPTER 5

Franz Stangl sat alone in his quarters. He drank from a large glass of brandy. It was his daily medicine, the only way he survived his assignment at Treblinka. He missed his wife terribly, and his children. He missed his beloved Austria. *If only I could receive a transfer!* Stangl often thought.

His uniform was pressed and laid on the table, ready for tomorrow. His boots were already shined. The brandy helped him not to dwell too deeply on any of the events of the day. He was happy for his workers; not only did they receive many delicious packages of food out of the Prague train, there were thousands of suitcases to sort through over the next few days and weeks. He was glad to be able to keep them employed and fully occupied; these duties meant life to his workers.

He also knew that idle hands were the cause of many troubles, so his goal as the *kommandant* was to make sure everyone kept working. As long as there were mountains of clothing to bundle in the sorting yard, then there would be Jewish workers running here and there all day, every day. He would walk around and inspect them. He would pretend that he cared about his assignment…that he was happy to be at Treblinka. He had made many changes for the better at the camp because that was who he was, a stickler for neatness and organization. But the camp had not always been so organized.

Stangl recalled on his first visit to Treblinka, when approaching the perimeter of the camp, he was astounded at all the dead bodies along the side of the road. He was also startled by the stench. The smell of decomposing bodies made him want to vomit. For some unknown reason, the corpses were left to rot in the hot sun, all along the tracks for the last kilometer before the gate to Treblinka.

Inside Treblinka's main gate Stangl was shocked to discover hundreds of dead bodies littered all across the unloading platform. *It was Dante's Inferno!* When Stangl walked away from his car toward the camp proper, international currency of various denominations flowed around his feet. At one side of the yard was a large mound with over a thousand rotting corpses. It was Dante come to life!

Stangl did not stay long at Treblinka on his first visit; his senses could not stand it. Everything at the camp was disorganized; it went against his highly structured concept of how to do police work and how concentration camps should be run. The man in charge obviously had no discipline. Stangl traveled to headquarters to see Odilo Globocnik at once. He remembered their conversation in vivid detail.

"I cannot do what you have assigned me to do," Stangl declared.

"Why not?" growled Globocnik.

"It is an impossible task. You would need a large work crew there for a month to make an impact. It is the end of the world there!"

"It is supposed to be an end of the world for *them*!" Globocnik rebuked. He was in charge of all the top-secret camps in Poland, with his mission coming straight from Heinrich Himmler. He needed followers to acquiesce, not cause problems. Mission accomplishment was all he desired, not sentimentality.

Beneath Globocnik's countenance was a bedrock of antagonism brittle enough to bust the drill bits of reasonable appeal, but Stangl tried again anyway. "I would like to transfer back to Austria. You don't understand…the mess of things there…at Treblinka." Stangl's tone held slightly less resolve. It was beginning to sink in that he was not being given a choice. Globocnik would not permit him to leave Poland. Stangl would be forced to work for Globocnik until the war was over; he simply knew too much.

Globocnik shook his doughy face and gave Stangl a cynical smile. "Get a room for yourself for the night and we will discuss it all in the morning. You will then travel back to Treblinka tomorrow to see what can be done. What Treblinka needs is a good organizer. You can do that for me. We will talk about it tomorrow. Dismissed."

Clearing his head from the memory, Franz Stangl finished his glass of brandy and decided to write a letter to his wife.

My dear Theresa,

How are you today? I have lived another uneventful day here at Treblinka. I get up in the morning, I walk my rounds, I do the paperwork, and in all these things there is something desperately missing and nagging in my mind, and it is you. I miss you very much. The sun shined brightly today but it was cool this morning, a beautiful day it would be if I was not here and away from you. Please squeeze Brigitte and Renate for me. I miss them so. I look forward to my leave in a few weeks. Please write. It has been almost two weeks since I have heard from you. There is not much entertainment here to pass the boredom. We do our jobs and then go to bed. I am thinking of making some gardens and perhaps a zoo next spring, if I am still here.

Your Paul

Pajamas on, he crawled into his silk sheets and softly pounded his goose down pillow a few times before he laid down his head. He would inspect Camp 2 tomorrow and make sure they were staying on schedule. *The camps must always be in top shape.*

CHAPTER 6

Rudi Masarek could not find it within himself to speak casually to the others for several days. He was in such intense pain—like an automaton doing the daily work without a soul.

Hans Freund, despite losing his only son and wife, seemed to pull himself together more quickly. He spoke to the others in the barracks at night, but they could see he was in a state of shock. His nervousness conveyed a lack of acceptance; he had not yet come to terms with Treblinka. It took several nights before they first heard him weep…when the evil facts seared his emotions. After his outpouring of anguish, Hans was better. He was depressed, but also more *settled*.

Besides the excruciating trauma of dealing with their loved ones' deaths, the simple act of sleeping in the male dormitory was also a challenge. Every evening several men would kill themselves. Others, merely trying to endure until the next day, heard the gasps and commotion from the suicide attempts, which occasionally failed. Sometimes it was a father and son, sometimes two best friends. One morning twenty men were carried out of the large barracks because of suicide. Grappling with the reality of Treblinka was too much for them.

Rudi and Hans were not absolutely sure that their wives were dead. There was a possibility that the two women had been pulled out of the disrobing area or the tube, but the odds were slim and they knew it. They had searched among the female workers who were launderers and cooks, and even asked them if they had seen their wives, all to no avail. They had very little hope, and every day their situation grew bleaker. However, none of the Jewish workers knew exactly what transpired on the other side of the sandy berm where Camp 2 was located. The Czech Jews were told that once a worker stepped foot in Camp 2 they were never allowed to depart from it. Camp 2 housed the darkest secrets of Treblinka.

All the Jewish workers had specific jobs to do. Carpenters, bricklayers, tailors, dentists, cobblers, bakers, doctors, and even musicians were spared to contribute their gifts to camp life. Rudi was assigned to the tailor shop and worked under an SS guard named Franz Suchomel. Richard and Karel reported each day to the sorting warehouse, working mostly with men's clothing. They were humorously referred to as "Karel and Richard from Men's Better Overcoats." Hans usually worked with Rudi, but sometimes worked in the sorting warehouse. Robert worked with Dr. Chorazycki, originally a nose and throat doctor, but currently working as an emergency room physician for those coming down with typhus fever caused by lice.

One Friday, however, they were all scheduled to work together. A shipment of five thousand Jews was coming in the morning and needed to be processed quickly because another shipment of close to seven thousand was coming in the afternoon. At five in the morning they were awakened by an alarm and given hard, dark bread and hot, artificial coffee in a tin cup. At six o'clock the *kapo* in charge formed the men in columns in the roll-call yard, called the *appelplatz*. When both the living and those dead from suicide were counted and the number was verified as accurate, they were released to march to their duty assignment.

The five Czech men were tasked to work at the sorting site near the wooden barracks where women and children were to be undressed and sheared. Two of the guards, Miete and Kuttner, were especially hard on the Jewish workers that morning, hitting them on their backs with whips and swearing at them, threatening to bring them to the *Lazarette*. Miete shot one Jew in the chest to prove his point—a warning to all of the workers that they were just as expendable as those coming off the transports.

Hans asked Robert why they were not going up near the tracks to help process the passengers.

"Because we are newcomers," Robert stated matter-of-factly. "Only the blue bands are allowed to go there because of the intensity of it. Same with the red armbands in the barracks with the women."

"What do you mean?" asked Hans.

"Not everyone can do it. Some of our brothers were tasked to help disrobe the women and cut their hair, but they wept and told the women the truth—that they were going to their deaths. The guards don't appreciate that. And for the blue bands, you can't imagine what a regular processing is like until a group from the east arrives. The guards use whips, and rifles, along with the Doll's attack dog to motivate people."

"You have a guard named the Doll?" inquired Hans.

"Yes. He was given that nickname because he has the face like that of a porcelain doll with sparkling eyes. His actual name is Kurt Franz and he is the second in command. Most of the guards have nicknames here—you'll learn. Kuttner is called Kiewe. Miete is known as the Angel of Death. These three are mental deviants; they are the worst here—all sadists!

"There's also an evil SS guard named Mentz who manages the *Lazarette*. All the guards whip us workers and resort to violence. It's as if they have to try to outdo one another when in charge. None of the guards want to appear weak. When trains come in from the west, rich with food, furs, and other valuables, the Nazis treat the passengers well to disguise what this place really is. They also pick more men out of the trains as they did with you and Rudi."

"Which guard is in charge?"

"A man named Franz Stangl, but he is not technically a guard. He is the *kommandant*, and was brought here from Sobibor to get Treblinka functioning well—essentially he is a Nazi pig, but I have never seen him hurt anybody. He just stands there and watches while work is being done, approving. You'll see him walk around the camp with a white coat and riding pants. He also sometimes stands on the berm and watches the naked souls run through the tube to their deaths. A very odd man, if you care to know my feelings."

"So every one of those passengers except Rudi and me, and a few others, all disappeared from the earth last week?"

"I'm sorry to say but, yes. And believe me, there will be thousands more today. Unfortunately that's why we're here."

Hans was thunderstruck.

★ ★ ★ ★ ★   ★ ★ ★ ★ ★

The morning train arrived and unloaded its passengers, creating pandemonium at Treblinka. Guards shouted. Jewish workers ran every which way for hours, carrying clothing, shoes, foodstuffs, and baggage. Over five thousand passengers were deposited into the Treblinka courtyard that morning. Several naked men were pulled out for work assignments and told to redress themselves.

The number of men selected for work was very close to the number of those who had committed suicide or were beaten to death the day before by the Doll, Miete, or Kiewe. The *kommandant* made sure that Treblinka did not surpass a certain number of Jewish laborers—three hundred workers in the upper "secret" camp and seven hundred workers in the lower camp where the men stood now.

Rudi and Hans fit right in with the other Czechs. When told to carry clothing from the unloading platform to the sorting area, they ran side by side. When told to sort the clothing and make bundles, which would eventually be loaded onto trains, they worked fastidiously together to get more done than what the guards would expect. The newcomers asked questions about Treblinka when the guards were not watching, so the three *veterans* educated them on the ways of the camp.

"Why do we keep hearing shots at the infirmary?" asked Hans. A building with a large red cross painted on it sat to the far right of the unloading area.

"You mean the *Lazarette*?"

"They are one and the same?"

"Yes."

"Then why did they put a red cross on it if it is to murder people?"

"Think about it! These men are con artists. Always duping the stupid masses. Believe me, if the people knew what they were really getting into when they alighted the train, there would be a revolt."

"The *Lazarette* is where the smell is coming from," explained Richard. "That is where we take the infirmed. It is disguised as a field hospital, but in reality it is an execution yard. We have heard that victims sit on a bench that is located alongside a trench and one of the SS guards, usually Mentz, walks behind them and puts a bullet in their neck. The body falls into the trench and is burned. Sometimes the shot doesn't kill the victim and they end up being burned alive. Trust me, you never want to go there."

"Who gets taken there?"

"Old and crippled people from the trains, those of us laborers who are caught stealing, and people who receive a scar on their face by one of the guards. The wound is called being *marked* because rival guards will do it to each other's protégés."

"Who are the protégés?"

"All of us are," answered Richard. "Whoever picked you out of line; even the evil Miete has protégés. They are all jealous of each other, and if they think one worker is especially liked by his *mentor*, then that gives them all the more reason to inflict harm on him."

Hans shook his head and muttered, "This is crazy!"

★ ★ ★ ★ ★   ★ ★ ★ ★ ★

The mountains of underwear, dresses, pants, shoes, and other items were tall enough to cast large shadows from the rising sun. Rudi, Hans, and the other Czechs worked feverishly throughout the morning to fold and bind all the clothes. By the end of the morning the colossal stockpiles were dented by their efforts but still towered over them by at least five feet.

Men's shirts, trousers, coats, and shoes were all inspected to determine if they were of good quality. If they passed the test, they were delivered to the tailor shop where the yellow Star of David was cut off and the garment mended so that it looked like it had never been there. They were placed on a special rack in the storeroom where the Nazis and Ukrainians could *shop*, though no money was exchanged.

All of the other clothing was bundled into cubes and hauled to the far side of the sorting yard, where there were wooden poles with signs on them placed at ten-meter intervals: RAGS, SILKS, COTTON, WOOL. The freshly made bundles—or cubes—were carefully placed on top of each other until little pyramids were formed. Prisoners would climb on top and reach down to continue to stack the clothing higher and higher. Eventually, when trains came to deliver goods west toward Germany, the bundles would be hauled to the platform and loaded onto the railcars.

While the Czechs worked hard folding clothes and making bundles, they noticed that the Jewish workers who had been at Treblinka longer were very carefully checking every seam and waistline of the clothing. Often, money and other valuables were found. They were told to put any and all paper bills and gold into designated suitcases; however, the Czechs noticed the older workers were stealthily passing items to each other as they were hauling the clothing cubes up to those on top.

Their old foreman, a deeply blue-eyed gentleman named David Brat, quietly explained to the Czechs that on the next train back to Warsaw, two men would stowaway inside the pyramid of clothes in an attempt to warn those in the ghetto about what was happening at Treblinka. If the men were successfully smuggled out of the camp, they would need lots of gold for bribes along the way to buy their way back into the ghetto.

This information was exhilarating for the newcomers to hear…that something hopeful was happening. "But how do you account for the discrepancy in the daily roll call?" asked Robert, who was scientifically minded.

Bucktoothed David explained, "We have camp elder Galewski in on it." Marceli Galewski was a former engineer from Lodz and looked up to by the workers. The Nazis trusted him to speak for the laborers and they held him responsible for the daily count.

David continued. "He changes the count between the morning and evening rolls so it looks like the two were never missing. If he is ever questioned about it, he explains that Miete took a couple of workers to the *Lazarette* that day. His excuse is always accepted."

"How do you get them on the trains?"

"We create a distraction. We have enough *kapos* on our side, and with Galewski vouching for us it has worked. We sent two away several days ago and it was never detected. So far, we have been lucky."

The Czech men watched from the corners of their eyes all the movement in the camp: SS guards yelling, *kapos* working to maintain order, and then the streams of women and children pouring out from the unloading platform and running toward the large processing barracks. It was hard, as men, not to run over and try to warn or help them. It took everything in them to stand fast, watching these helpless children, mothers, and grandmothers—their people—unknowingly enter the building where they would strip and have their hair cut.

The Jewish workers could hear the cries from the women in the tube while they were prodded by men with whips. The men knew the women and children must be intensely frightened, wondering what would happen to them. Conceivably, the workers gave those passing through the camp false hope that so many of the men were bundling clothes and helping in the barn, acting as if nothing terrible was happening. *Perhaps this is truly a work camp!* As soon as the large diesel engine started up again, the Czech men noticed dozens of large suitcases departing the sorting barn containing the women's hair. It made them feel hollow.

After that would come the naked men who had been detained on the platform to undress. They poured through the long rectangular warehouse, passing the same place where their wives, daughters, and mothers had their hair brusquely sheared off, and then they were ordered to run through the back door and into the tube to meet the same fate as thousands of others that day.

The Czechs realized what a very organized procedure the Nazis had created. From emptying people out of the railcars where they were threatened and hurried down the platform and into the large wooden barracks, then yelled at to go through the back-door opening toward the tube. There was nowhere left to run once inside the front door of the barracks. Unless one or two were called out for laundry or cooking duty, all who entered perished. No children were ever called out, the Czechs learned, much to the agony of Hans.

The Jewish workers received a thirty-minute rest break for lunch. The Czechs gathered together under a large pine tree at the far side of the sorting area. They held their tin plates and cups while their eyes scanned the yard, hoping to be left alone from the Doll, Miete, or Kiewe.

Hours later, the Czech men finally cleared all of the women's clothing out of the wooden barracks building and were bundling it for departure on the next westbound train. They didn't have long to wait as they heard another locomotive entering Treblinka station. They were told to stop sorting and to help with the tightly packed train of thirty railcars because there were not enough blue bands to complete the task before dark.

And the same scene played out once again. The new passengers were ushered out of the railcars and processed away from the unloading platform. This time, however, the Czech men helped carry dead bodies to the *Lazarette* to be burned, and then they swept out the railcars of all the blood and excrement. Each car had to be inspected to ensure it was clean before it was reloaded with supplies and departed Treblinka.

There was an eerie feeling among the Czechs that afternoon, disbelief that all the people who had run past them could have actually gone to their deaths. *Could there be another work farm, miles away, where the passengers were shipped after their showers? Could there be another destiny for them?* Yet they knew it couldn't be so. There were no trains or busses leading away from Camp 2, and the only noise coming from there, after the screaming in the tube, was a loud tank motor. That day the motor ran all morning, all afternoon, and well into the evening, when it was finally turned off after dark.

Before the Czechs were locked in for the night, they lined up with approximately one hundred other men as the guards inspected their barracks. In one of the cots an SS guard discovered a large chunk of a ham. Miete, with his thick neck and broad face, confronted the men in the courtyard, threatening that if someone did not confess who took it and from precisely where the ham came, then all would be shot.

One Polish man stepped forward and said it was his ham, and that he had stolen it from the Ukrainians. Immediately afterward, another Pole stepped forward and said the first man was lying, that it was actually his ham, and that he had bought it from a Ukrainian guard because it was his birthday. Further, he said he would willingly go to the *Lazarette*.

The Czech men were stunned by the man's honesty, but Miete would have none of it. He separated out the birthday boy's entire row—five men—and marched them all to the *Lazarette*. After positioning them on the wooden bench, one by one they were shot and fell into the flames of the ever-burning pit. The last man, the one who had confessed about his birthday ham, accidentally slid off the bench and laid on the side of the pit. When the shot to terminate his life was delayed, he yelled out to Miete, "Hurry up! Why don't you shoot, for goodness sake?"

The shot never came. He was instructed to get back up, depart the *Lazarette*, and rejoin the other men as they entered the male barracks. The man who had turned another year older that day stood up, walked out of the pit, and, with uncontrollable shaking, passed by Miete, departing the villainous area where his kind and faithful comrades would forever remain.

CHAPTER 7

Tchechia had been at Treblinka for several weeks. During that time, she had eaten better at the camp but had still lost weight from all the running and working from dawn until dusk. She worked first in the laundry, washing the linens of the Nazi overlords and the Ukrainian guards. She and three other young women also washed items from the kitchen and were often asked to either help the mess staff during meals or attend to patients in the small medical clinic. Tchechia's distinctive blond hair drew the attention of the SS guards, but she was mostly left alone by the workforce of the camp.

The job she liked the best—though not assigned to her very often—was sweeping the SS quarters and emptying their trash. Tchechia felt it was her duty to try to spy on the Nazis to see if she could discover anything about the war, or about the future of the concentration camp where she worked. Once, she found a newspaper left open on the *kommandant*'s desk. She could not make out all the German words, but she determined it was about the war in Stalingrad, and that the Germans were stalled out and not making much progress.

Bronka was managing to get by as a seamstress and performed limited tailoring. She worked alongside Rudi Masarek and several other Jewish men who had been chosen out of a transport to perform camp labor. Rudi was a master with clothing since he had worked in the shirt business with his father in Prague. He taught Bronka trade skills since she had never worked as a seamstress before.

"You are much more talented than I will ever be," said Bronka.

"You will learn," Rudi responded to her in a kind tone. "The important thing to remember is to keep one eye just ahead of where you are stitching so you do not veer off course and make a mistake."

"Like I have already done a few times," said Bronka with a slight smile.

Bronka appreciated Rudi's kindness to her. She knew he was in similar despair as she, mourning the loss of loved ones. At first Bronka thought that perhaps her parents and siblings could be somehow working in Camp 2, and that maybe she would see them again. But as time marched on and every day she continued to see the masses pour out of the trains, stripped, chased down the tube by guards with whips, and no sign of any of these thousands of people, she knew only one fate had befallen her family.

Bronka felt encouraged by Rudi while at work, but she realized that he had his own emotional stressors. Everyone at Treblinka mourned the loss of loved ones. It was especially hard for her at night before going to sleep, when she had time to think about her family. She wept just after lights-out, before she slept, as she thought of her younger sisters and sweet mother. One of the women in her barracks hanged herself to escape the pain. Bronka was slightly envious of her, yet she recognized she herself did not have the capacity to end her life that way.

Rudi had confided in Bronka that there may be a day coming when they could escape, and this gave her some hope. He whispered to her one day, "Remember to always feel the fabric for aberrations where there might be gold. We are saving it to help those who escape."

"Who gets to escape?" asked Bronka. She was encouraged for the first time since she could remember.

"No one who would be obvious to the guards," Rudi answered. "We can only send out people they have not noticed, those who stand at the back of the formation. In this way we can fake the numbers for the head count without them knowing. I don't think any women could be sent out because there are too few of you. Suchomel would know immediately that you had escaped if you did not show up for work in the morning."

Rudi and Bronka worked for a thirty-five-year old SS guard named Franz Suchomel, who had previously served in Germany's euthanasia program, and of this fact he reminded his team often. It was a veiled threat. Suchomel was not as physically abusive as some of the other guards such as Miete or Kuttner, but he kept discipline with verbal threats and attempted to guilt the Jewish workers into performing well for the camp. Rudi and Bronka did not feel *liked* by Suchomel, but he tolerated them more than the others, and tried to protect his team from the more sadistic guards. However, he failed to give them what they so desperately craved: reason to believe they would survive Treblinka.

★ ★ ★ ★ ★   ★ ★ ★ ★ ★

Bronka spoke to Tchechia at night and told her about the escape plans being worked on by Rudi and some of the other men.

"I wish I could leave tonight," said Tchechia one evening. "I cannot stand the way the guards all look at me. I don't think I will last much longer."

"I am sure that it can't be tonight," said Bronka thoughtfully. "Rudi said there are too few of us women, that it would be too obvious if one of us vanished. With the men, if the head count is questioned at the end of the day, they just lie and explain that the Doll or Miete sent someone to the *Lazarette*. But that wouldn't work for us."

"Maybe one day there will be a revolt," said Tchechia. "Until then, I will continue to look for ways to steal secrets from the guards. They do not realize that as they watch me, I am also watching them. I see their patterns, when they are gone and how frequently."

"Be careful, Tchechia!" warned Bronka. "Don't cross them, and don't stare back at them. They will hurt you."

"I want to kill these pigs, every last one of them. They are murderers and deceivers. You know, they tell the women that the water is getting cold so they must hurry down the tube. They also have the Star of David above the bathhouse door so that people are not afraid—the liars!"

"Please be careful," said Bronka. "I don't know what I would do without you."

★ ★ ★ ★ ★   ★ ★ ★ ★ ★

One day, Tchechia reported to work at the infirmary to assist Dr. Chorazycki, the fifty-seven-year-old camp physician. When she walked into the room, the doctor took a good look at her and said, "You do not look Semitic."

Tchechia attempted a smile that failed and replied, "I've been told that before." She tried to keep in stride with the doctor as he walked through the small clinic, checking on his patients, most of whom had typhus. "You are the opposite of me; you look Jewish, but I hear you are not," said Tchechia.

"I was born Jewish," countered Chorazycki, "but I converted to Catholicism as an adult."

"Why are you here?" asked Tchechia. She wondered about this man who, according to Bronka, was complicit with the men organizing escapes.

"Already a doctor, I was *procured* by the Russians during the great war. Then I was a captain and chief physician in the Polish army during the Bolshevik war. During peacetime, I started a private practice in Warsaw. My family and I worked to help rebuild our sovereign nation. For thanks I was forced into the ghetto, and lived there for over a year. You know the rest," he said soberly, connecting eyes with her for an instant.

Tchechia nodded.

"We are the lucky ones," he declared sarcastically, glancing away again.

Tchechia thought about what he said. She felt that she herself was just beginning at life, but he had already lived a full one. Unfortunately they were both at Treblinka at the same point in time. *And would likely never leave,* she thought.

Tchechia wondered about this man, so confident in his medical skills and his worldview. He had seen so much, yet he was forced to work for sixteen hours a day in a cramped infirmary, never knowing which day might be his last. She found it admirable that he kept a strong, defiant attitude.

Over time, Tchechia grew fond of Dr. Chorazycki and was always glad when asked to work in the infirmary. She felt the doctor also liked it when she helped him. This made Tchechia happy and gave her something to look forward to. But there was something in his actions, and in his tone when he spoke. Something desperate. She knew that, like Bronka's Rudi, the doctor would be important if there was an uprising.

CHAPTER 8

Franz Stangl walked over to the SS table carrying his white porcelain plate filled with meats, small potatoes, cauliflower, and fresh bread. He sat across from his deputy, Kurt Franz, along with August Miete, Willi Mentz, Franz Suchomel, and Kurt Kuttner. No one spoke while they put their first few bites into their mouths. It was a long day, having processed so many prisoners.

Stangl had taken his beautiful mare for a ride around the countryside that morning. It was one of the few pleasures he enjoyed at the camp. It reminded him of when he was a young man, before the war, and before he had ever heard of the name Treblinka.

He had seen good times and bad times throughout his life. Working with a man named Christian Wirth at the euthanasia center at Hartheim was terrible. He had met coarse men before, but Wirth was absolutely foul and degenerate. Some of the other leaders had put Stangl's mind at ease when he arrived at Hartheim. He was told the patients being euthanized were carefully selected by a team of physicians as unrecoverable. Wirth, however, countered all of their words as sentimental rubbish. "We must do away with useless mouths!" Wirth would proclaim. Stangl was thankful he was in charge of Treblinka, and Wirth was miles away. But dealing with subordinates could also be a challenge.

Stangl finally started the conversation. "I have spent some time at the upper camp today. They are running out of room for their work. I called Globocnik. He said if we have no more room we are going to have to start burning."

The Germans sitting around Stangl gave a slight moan at the thought of it.

"How?" asked his number two, also known by the camp workers as the

Doll. "We do not have a crematorium. It is easy to say something from a distance, but Globocnik is not here having to manage it."

"We are going to have the workers make ovens, essentially large roasting pits," said Stangl. "It will be quite an operation. They will probably need more men there to get this up and going. A crematorium will be built eventually, but until then we will use the roasting pits."

"And what do we do with all the ash?" Kuttner asked. He was a staff sergeant in charge of day-to-day operations. Before his tenure at Treblinka, he had worked as chief of police at a German military prison.

"Spread it around," replied Stangl evenly. "The workers will have to devise a way to blend it into the earth. Perhaps a layer of ash, a layer of soil. Have them experiment. Or we could take wagonloads down to the river, but I would prefer to keep it in the fields."

The men continued to eat their meals, thinking of the upcoming change to operations. They all knew it would bring an unbearable stench to both camps. Working at Treblinka would become all the more a hardship tour if they were forced to smell death every day.

"There is something else," continued Stangl. "It is time to tweak our practices with the workers." Before he could get out his next words he noticed an eye roll from Miete. "What I mean to say is that since operations are running smoothly, it would be good to keep most of the workers we have now." Stangl could tell by their faces that they wanted more explanation.

"They are specialists. They have overcome the shock of arriving at Treblinka and are useful to us. For instance, the gold Jews. They are craftsmen. We need to keep them around." Stangl then glanced at Suchomel, who ran the tailor shop. "I hear there are some tailors who are quite skilled. We also have a Viennese baker who made us this fine bread tonight. I want to keep him."

"We have a concentration camp to run, and that requires discipline," said Kuttner carefully.

"I realize that more than any of you, and infractions, of course, will not be tolerated," countered Stangl. "But for the day-to-day operations we want to keep most of the workers we have."

"This is how revolts happen," cautioned Kuttner. "If we keep the same prisoners together for a period of a time, they form relationships and begin to trust each other. Routinely moving them around and making examples out of them is how we keep them loyal and obedient."

Stangl waved his hand a little at Kuttner as if he was annoyed. Then staring down at his food, he said, "Just humor me. Let's keep the majority of the workers we have. They are serving us well. I hear we have recruited two concert violinists and an operatic tenor from Warsaw. Let's keep them! Perhaps we can have a concert. These workers know their jobs and perform them quickly. Just cut back on anything unnecessary, that's all. Cut back."

The other officers all left en masse, having a few words with each other outside the mess building. Stangl knew it would be hard for a couple of them to adapt, but they hopefully got the point. He wanted efficiency, even at the risk of an uprising, which was minimal at most. In order to have a revolt the Jewish workers would need strong leadership, something impossible in a place like Treblinka.

CHAPTER 9

S oon after Rudi and Hans arrived, another former Czech army officer alighted onto the rail platform. His name was Zelo Bloch. Out of five thousand people on the morning train, Zelo was the only man chosen by the SS to stay and work; the other men were stripped and departed down the tube. Zelo's young wife was also not chosen, and after a piercing look into her husband's eyes she ran into the wooden barracks and was never seen by him again.

That night, the Czech men invited Zelo to bunk in their area. When it came time for lights-out, Zelo asked them about the passengers who were not selected to work. Richard cleared his throat and began to share with Zelo what most likely happened to his wife once she was out of his sight. The other men were curious what the newcomer would say, or if he would weep, but Zelo remained calm. The lights were turned out and they could not hear him whimper.

Richard continued. "This is not a work camp, Zelo."

"I understand," Zelo said softly.

They were his last words of the evening, and he was lying.

★ ★ ★ ★ ★   ★ ★ ★ ★ ★

Zelo was unique in that the Nazis did not need any additional workers on the specific morning he was picked out of the line. It was most definitely his brute strength and magnificent strong jaw the Nazis noticed. Zelo looked like a winner with his flowing black hair and mustache. Thankfully for the Czech contingent, not only did Zelo look like a leader, he brought with him a military mind, a winsome personality, and a forcefulness the group did not know they were missing until he arrived.

There were designated leaders, such as camp elder Galewski, but

Zelo quickly became the one from whom others drew strength. People trusted him. His attributes made Zelo their leader, not only of the Czech contingent, but of the entire male barracks. It was not just his looks and mannerisms; it was something deeper, intangible, and it gave Zelo much respect. There was a lot to adore about Zelo: he honestly cared for other people and looked them in the eye when speaking to them. Because of this, people bestowed authority on him and looked up to him for leadership.

While all the Czech men had befriended Zelo at once, it was Robert who became the closest to him. The two men became thick as thieves. Zelo was the idea man who brought strength, will, and determination. Robert was the intellectual who thought everything through and analyzed the individual pieces. With this combination, it wasn't long before all the Czech men were conspiring about escaping from Treblinka.

"So what is the situation here?" asked Zelo, his brown eyes shining in the candlelight.

Richard started. "We have seen several people escape in ones or twos to send word back to Warsaw regarding what this camp is all about. We are able to smuggle from the luggage almost as much gold and currency as we need to bribe the Ukrainian guards. But they are sometimes not very dependable."

"What about weapons?" Zelo was obviously thinking larger than just one or two.

"All the extra weapons and explosives are stored in the arms room," said Robert. "However, the challenge is that it is located right next door to where the Germans sleep. If we do anything, it will have to be during the day and include a decoy operation."

"Any sympathizers among the Germans?" asked Zelo hopefully.

"Not really," said Karel. "There are some who don't beat us as badly as the psychopaths, but there are no trustworthy Germans, if that's what you mean."

"What about key people in the workers' group?"

"We have Galewski who is honorable and we can trust," Karel answered. "He has already had a positive influence, helping with the escapes so far."

"There is Dr. Chorazycki who I work with," said Robert. "He hates all the Nazis and has already spoken to me about a revolt. He said that he will do whatever he can to help if there is a plan. Plus, the SS come to him for medical attention and to seek his advice, so if the SS trust him then he will be able to help us."

"That's good," said Zelo. "We need to plan a larger-scale assault on the camp leadership. Regarding the weapons, do you think we can get a key made for the arms room somehow?"

The question itself injected a shot of excitement into the small group.

Rudi, as if awakened from a dream, answered with a gleam in his blue eyes, "I will check it out and see what I can do about the key."

"Excellent!" said Zelo. "On the day of the grand revolt, we will cut their phone lines and somehow barricade the entrance to prevent reinforcements from coming. If we take all of their weapons, we could do quite a lot of damage. I think that if we unite together, not just a few of us, but the entire group, we could kill most of the SS and guards, and then escape into the woods beyond this camp. Every night let's meet to tally our inventory of what we have stolen and discuss how we have progressed with our strategy."

The men looked at each other with new hope and resolve. Their minds were forced to think about the necessity and reality of actually escaping, and what that would be like. The workers all understood that the guards were liars; the promise that they might live to see their freedom did not hold any truth. Treblinka was a killing machine. No one who was ever sent to Treblinka could escape it. The Jewish workers had been told by one of the guards the camp was a top-secret mission, and each of the SS were handpicked for this assignment.

Robert speculated that perhaps it was not only the workers who were in danger of being eliminated but also the guards. He wondered if at some point, when Treblinka ever ran out of Jews to kill and had to close down, that Hitler might also kill all the SS and Ukrainian guards, simply to cover up his tracks and hide his dirty secrets. Perhaps no one was ever meant to live after Treblinka.

Their breakaway plan to disarm and kill the guards was something they enjoyed thinking about—the death of the Doll, Kiewe, Miete, and Mentz. Unfortunately it could mean their own deaths as well. Zelo's conviction that they should all escape in a grand revolt brought them a hope they had not held since their arrival. It *must* be possible.

They had heard about prison uprisings before in their history classes. The key, they knew, was to catch their captors unawares. If any of the SS or the Ukrainians were to suspect their plans, or worse, catch any of them storing money or weapons, great reprisals would surely follow—perhaps even a mass execution like none that had previously been seen. While Zelo brought great hope to the men, his plans also brought increased risk. All these thoughts swirled around in their heads for hours after lights-out.

CHAPTER 10

Reveille, and early morning roll call on the *appelplatz*.
Report to assigned positions.

Hear a locomotive enter Treblinka station.

Listen to the gunshots and screaming from the loading platform.

See the men and women separated, then forced to undress and run down the tube.

Handle the new clothing and valuables.

Gather everything together into bundles to ship.

The violent days at Treblinka all took on the same form. It was an endless barrage of chaos, carnage, and monotony. But there was something new happening in Camp 2 that was impacting everyone. The Czech contingent heard that Jewish workers in the upper camp were forced to build tremendous roasting pits to burn the bodies taken out of the shower chambers. Depending on the wind direction, a horrible stench would sometimes permeate every part of the main work camp. A few of the Jewish workers vomited as they ran doing their chores.

Richard, Karel, Hans, and Zelo reported to the sorting work detail. The passengers to be processed that day came from Western Europe and were loaded with valuables, usually hidden in secret pockets or knapsacks. Myriads of supplies were formed into piles in the sorting yard:

lighters in one pile,

compacts in another,

soaps,

matches,

silver pens in one pile and gold pens in another,

silver watches,

gold watches,
and one platinum watch pocketed by a work Jew for a future bargain with
a Ukrainian.
Wallets here,
belts there,
flashlights in a pile of their own.
Bottles are organized together by color.
All currency was stuffed into different suitcases;
zloty in one,
marks in another,
francs in a third,
and guilders in a fourth.

An additional suitcase was available for diamonds, which was guarded
by an SS, who kept reminding the workers not to pocket anything or they
would be shot in the neck by Mentz at the *Lazarette*.

Despite being eyed suspiciously throughout the day by various guards,
the Czechs were able to pocket quite a bit of currency and diamonds they
found hidden in the clothing, and even in some loaves of bread. On Zelo's
orders, everyone was to bring as many valuables as possible each night to
their meeting to be used for the future uprising.

Zelo Bloch began to work not only with the other Czechs, but with
camp elder Galewski. Zelo learned that Galewski was already devising a
plan for a unified revolt, whereby both camps would participate in a coor-
dinated attack, something Zelo had thought impossible since there was no
communication between Camp 1 and Camp 2. Galewski told Zelo there
was a specialized carpenter named Jankiel Wiernik who was tasked with
construction projects at both camps. Jankiel would deliver messages back
and forth from Galewski to those in Camp 2 who were committed to a
revolt—with Jankiel being one of them.

"I was told that no one who steps foot in Camp 2 is allowed to leave,"
Zelo stated.

"Jankiel is special," said Galewski. "A master workman, and the Nazis
need him too much…in both camps. To my knowledge, he is the only one

with this privilege. Let us hope he continues to hold their favor, otherwise we are totally cut off from those in Camp 2."

The Czech men were encouraged with this information, and were happy that Zelo had earned the confidence of Galewski. Knowing that both camps were part of the escape plan seemed to make a revolt more real, and that so many more of them might escape. Galewski routinely told Zelo that they could not leave their Camp 2 brothers alone to die with the horrible retaliation sure to follow.

In the meantime, Galewski helped to organize several escapes, some of which worked, and some of which did not. The gruesome reprisals were put on display for all to see, and take warning. Two men were found hiding underneath some tightly packed clothing bundles inside a train that was about to depart for Warsaw. The escapees were promptly whipped all the way to the courtyard where the other prisoners had been gathered as witnesses. The men were stripped, tied onto poles, and hung upside down, then whipped again and left on the poles until they perished.

On another occasion, when the Czech men's hopes were still high for escape, they were awakened earlier than normal for a special formation before sunrise. Seven blue-banded Jewish workers who helped on the platform had tried to make an escape. The previous night they stormed the guard at the camp gate nearest town in hopes of several making it past. But before they could overtake the guard he was able to call for help and several SS men came running. All seven prisoners were captured and put under guard for the rest of the night.

Just after roll call the seven blue-banded workers were brought to the front of the formation and the Doll stepped forward to speak to the camp.

"Today is the last day we will mete out a mild punishment," he declared. "From now on, every *kapo* and foreman will be directly liable with their own lives if any of their people try to escape. Also, ten men will be shot for every one person who escapes, or tries to escape. Do you understand? For one, ten others! This is very clear for you."

The Doll had the seven men transported to the infirmary to be shot in the neck and burned. But he made sure the *kapos* and foremen were all there to witness the execution.

When the job was done, Kurt Franz told the Jewish leaders, "It will not be worth it for you if it happens again. You will be done away with the same way. These are the new rules. Dismissed."

That same evening Galewski and Zelo conferred and decided that no more escapes should be attempted. They would focus their attention on the entire group departing after setting fire to the camp.

★ ★ ★ ★ ★   ★ ★ ★ ★ ★

Rudi Masarek dreamed of his wife Gisela. He could see her from a position nearby as she maneuvered through the large disrobing barracks and was ordered to take off her clothes. Now he was standing in the back of the building as Gisela was ushered into the room where she sat with her arms covering her breasts and screaming for Rudi to help her. He did not move; he could not speak.

Gisela's beautiful hair was quickly chopped four times by a work Jew with a red armband—once in the front, once in the back, and then a rough chop on each side. With no time to mourn for her hair, she was steered out the back door and into the tube with many other women.

Rudi slowly followed, as if drifting behind in a cloud as a ghost, watching as guards herded Gisela down the long path toward the showers. There was a bend in the pathway to the right and then a brick building loomed before those waiting in line. She pleaded with him, crying; she was ordered to raise her arms high above her head by the Nazis on the berm with machine guns. One of the SS guards was using a whip to position the women closer and closer to the brick building.

The heavy door of the building was opened; the women filed inside, shrieking. There was a Star of David just above their heads as they entered the building, but it was a mockery and offered them no protection. Gisela turned and gave one more glance at Rudi as she stepped into the brick building. Immediately, Rudi was in the low-ceilinged building with her, watching and still unable to speak. The women were shoved mercilessly into place until there was no more room and they were pressed against each other, tighter than on the rail trip. The door was sealed shut. There was a pause, silence, and all the women looked up to see an array of metal showerheads protruding from the ceiling, evenly spaced throughout the large room.

Gisela looked at Rudi and with her eyes pleaded with him to help, but his throat was dry, he could not speak, and his legs felt paralyzed. Moments of silent horror passed before a sound of a large diesel motor rumbled up to full capacity. The women watched the showerheads, but there was no water. Suddenly dark fumes and a pungent odor flooded the room. Choking, coughing, crying. Rudi could no longer see Gisela; there was simply a torrent of anguish and wailing while the gas worked its evil on the victims. One final rush of spewing anguish flooded the unconcerned structure before dissolving into an eerie silence.

Rudi startled awake, heart racing and mind exploding. He wanted to run over to the brick building to see if he could save Gisela. But his head cleared and he remembered that she was not there. His beloved wife had perished weeks earlier. He controlled his breathing. He thought of her sad eyes. He could still hear the cries, like screaming vultures in his mind. Blood hammered through his temples. As Rudi turned on his side in the darkness, he noticed a terrible odor that reminded him of what was happening in Camp 2.

PART 2

THE DOLL

CHAPTER 11

Kurt Franz walked onto the sorting yard and began randomly shoot-ing his pistol—aimed at head level—in a circle all around him. *Crack! Crack! Crack!* He finally emptied the revolver and began to reload it. Meanwhile, the Jewish workers fled in all directions to escape his wild entrance. Even the other SS and Ukrainian guards had to scramble out of the way. Typical of Franz, if not shooting when he arrived, he waved his whip and began hitting the first man he saw. It did not matter who the man happened to be, one sympathetic to the Nazis or to the Jewish workers. Franz wanted to punish people.

Franz believed he alone possessed the will necessary to keep Treblinka going. He understood what Stangl relayed to the officers a few days earlier about keeping the current loyal workers, but discipline must be main-tained. Besides, Globocnik and he were allies. In fact, he felt he worked for Globocnik more than he did for Stangl. Stangl sometimes appeared weak, and did not have a stomach for discipline. But Franz did, and he was bound to use it.

He walked toward the railroad platform where hundreds of Jews were unloading. He took a Ukrainian guard's rifle and told him, "You need to learn to use this thing."

Franz shot into one of the railroad cars as Jews were trying to step out. An older gentleman fell back into the car, dead amidst shrieks from those around him. Franz shot a little girl who had gotten separated from her mother. Then he aimed at one of the blue-banded Jewish workers and squeezed his trigger, watching the man fall forward into the crowd. Franz handed the rifle back to the guard.

"Use it," he said, while smiling.

Kurt Franz walked over to the mess hall where his dog Bari was waiting for him. After breakfast he would take Bari up to the platform and let him attack someone in the crowd. Franz knew the only way the Nazis succeeded over the Jews with inferior numbers was to put panic and fear into them as they were unloaded and herded into the tube. Franz prided himself on being the best at it, then Miete, and then Kuttner. Suchomel and some of the others were too lenient and soft, taking the guidance of the *kommandant*, which was not what Treblinka needed.

Franz ate in peace, reflecting on from where he had come just a few years before. At twenty-eight years of age he had seen a lot in his adult life. The son of a merchant, Franz was trained as a cook and then joined the SS and worked at the Buchenwald concentration camp. Because of his severity and competence there, he was recruited to help with euthanasia programs at several of the major centers where he *alleviated* a tremendous burden on society. Now he was at Treblinka, forced to deal with the continuous inpouring of Jews who were also destined to be purged from society.

Franz took his dog up to the unloading platform. Standing before one prestigious-looking Jewish man, Franz yelled, "Boy, sic the dog!"

The mongrel dog, which looked somewhat like a St. Bernard, went straight for the Jewish man's private area and tore into the defenseless soul with fury. Bari bit all around the man's midsection and then his face after the man fell to the ground. Once the attack subsided, Franz walked over to the man and pulled out his pistol. "Here you go," Franz said sarcastically while shooting the man in the neck. He then looked around for another vulnerable person for Bari to attack.

"You Jews started the war," Franz said mockingly. "You wanted the war. So now you have it."

Franz knew that what was most important was to command respect. He believed he held the most respect, not only among the workers but also the Ukrainian guards. Nobody wanted to interfere with him, and he relished that fact. The more daring he was while dealing with the Jewish workers unloading from the trains, the more people stood in awe of him, as if he possessed some kind of superhuman force. It was lost on him why the other SS and Ukrainian guards did not act the way he did.

He had considered everything very carefully; these people on the trains were going to their eventual death in the gas chamber. The more violent he was with them on the unloading platform, the less they would have to suffer later. He was doing them a great favor. Plus, he was putting fear into the masses, forcing them to run when the Nazis told them to run. He cherished efficiency.

Kurt Franz saw an elderly couple walking slowly and approached them.

"Please," he said to the couple nicely, "let me assist you. I can tell you would not do well running down to the showers. Let us lead you to the infirmary where you can get some rest after your long journey."

The surprised seniors glanced up at him with genuine warmth in their faces.

"Thank you," the grateful husband said.

"Not a problem," Franz replied. He then motioned with his hand and a blue band immediately ran over and stood before him at attention. "Take these two to the *Lazarette*. They have had a hard trip and need a break. Tell Corporal Mentz that I personally sent them to him."

As the couple walked off, the aging woman glanced back and smiled at Kurt Franz, but he didn't see her. Franz was walking with Bari toward a Jewish baby who had been placed on the ground beside the train.

CHAPTER 12

During their nightly meetings, Hans lamented, "We have to do something about the Doll!" He sat perched on his wooden bunk next to Zelo, Richard, Karel, Robert, and Rudi. The Czech men had peppered the mattress with gold and other goods to store for the revolt. "This morning he killed eleven men, including one of the blue bands helping to unload the passengers. I also heard he threw a baby against the side of the train. He is out of his mind and getting worse. Can we please deal with him before the revolt?"

The other men enjoyed thinking about eliminating Kurt Franz, but as everyone pondered it the startling reality was that they could not make any waves before the big day, the day they had been planning since Zelo arrived. It was Zelo who finally answered Hans.

"I understand, friend, but we must wait."

"Say that to the workers the Doll has killed this week," responded Hans emptily.

"The possibility of the revolt being successful diminishes greatly if we start changing the variables we are up against," said Robert, the theoretician of the group. "Taking out Stangl's deputy could put us on lockdown—or worse, a mass killing of all of us workers. Who knows? They might send twelve SS guards to replace him. Like Zelo said, we must wait."

"Look, Hans, I want him dead as much as you," said Richard, who was born in Prague and the son of a financial consultant. He was a student at the University of Prague until it shut down at the end of 1939 because of riots. "What I see each day eats me alive. Brothers of ours attacked by Bari or killed by Franz. He is a sadist, no doubt, but we must endure him until that one final moment. Then everything must be done at once, including his death."

"That's right," continued Robert, "and until that day we make ourselves look like we are in perfect shape, with shined boots, a nice pair of clothes, and a clean-shaven face. I think I shaved my face on the run six times today. We do all these things just for the privilege of not being taken by Miete into the *Lazarette* to let Mentz shoot us in the neck."

★ ★ ★ ★ ★   ★ ★ ★ ★ ★

Soon after that conversation, Hans was made a foreman like Zelo. They both worked for camp elder Galewski. At any one time there were usually a dozen *kapos* assigned to different operations within the camp. Two were in charge of the blue bands at the unloading platform. Two were in charge of the red bands in the undressing barracks, one was in charge of the kitchen and laundry, and several were stationed at the sorting yard where most of the Czech men worked.

There was a young, well-built *kapo* named Benjamin Rakowski, a handsome man who owned a farm before the war. Rakowski was the number two man to Galewski. One morning, immediately after roll call, the SS guard Miete, the Angel of Death, shouted at the formation, "All *kapos*, camp elders, and foremen are to immediately report to me."

Hans, Zelo, Galewski, Rakowski, and several other men stepped out of the formation, ran over to Sergeant Miete, and stood at attention. Miete had his hat pulled tightly down his forehead, so one could barely see his beady eyes. Whenever there was a change of protocol there was terror in the air, thinking that this might be the day when all the *kapos* would be liquidated and a new set picked. The men had no idea what the SS knew about their revolt plan, or if there might be a traitor among them. However, their greatest fears were not realized that morning.

"All right, it appears there is a need for more workers at Camp 2. I am going to allow you to pick out the volunteers. I want each of you to pick out two or three men, and remember what you've heard about Camp 2. Perhaps you should think about choosing the slackers in your group, or those who shirk their duties. I want twenty men standing before me in one minute, and if I don't, you *kapos* will make up the difference."

All of the Jewish supervisors quickly moved into the ranks of men and grabbed fellow prisoners as volunteers. There was a stifled protest, seen clearly in the eyes of the men chosen. Hans moved into the formation, stood just in front of Richard and Karel, and then picked the man standing immediately behind them. It was not hard to pick twenty men within a minute. The *kapos* knew which men they wanted to get rid of, men who were not as tightly bound to the escape plan as other men. However, they knew they had to pick young, strong men or else they would be sending them to their deaths.

The *kapos* heard from the carpenter Jankiel Wiernik that the men in Camp 2 were forced to run all day with heavy litters. Two to three corpses were expected to be carried at one time. If the men were not fast enough, or happened to drop the litter, they would be shot on the spot by one of the SS.

The twenty fresh recruits for Camp 2 were given one more minute to run back into the barracks to grab their belongings. Then they were marched off toward the upper camp by Miete. The Czech men were thankful they were not part of the volunteers this time, all because Zelo and Hans were looking out for them. The younger ones, Richard and Karel, breathed a sigh of relief, but knew it could happen any day. As Miete disappeared with his recruits, in the distance a train could be heard coming toward Treblinka station. Galewski told the group to hustle to their assigned places and get to work; it would be a long day with plenty of clothing and valuables to sort through before it was over.

★ ★ ★ ★ ★   ★ ★ ★ ★ ★

Kurt Franz escorted his dog Bari to the unloading platform and stood before a Jewish passenger who had just undressed and was holding his shoes, alongside hundreds of other naked men.

"Boy, sic the dog!" Franz yelled.

As the growling Bari lunged toward the newcomer, the man turned sideways so the dog would not attack his privates. Instead Bari took a bite of flesh out of the man's bottom, which sent the man tumbling forward, clinging to the back of another man. Bari lunged again and bit into the man's thigh. The pitiful victim tried to hide behind the other men standing around him.

All were terrified at what was happening, but Franz simply stood by and watched with an amused look on his face. When Bari finally resorted to a menacing growl without attacking, Franz stepped over the bleeding man, pulled out his pistol, and shot him in the neck. Two blue bands walked over and placed the man on a stretcher. Then they sprinted toward the *Lazarette*.

Franz decided to walk over to Camp 2 with Bari. He was wondering if the giant pyres were nearing completion to help enhance operations. He wanted to observe the work and to make sure they were ready for the morning's processing, much to the relief of all at Camp 1.

★ ★ ★ ★ ★   ★ ★ ★ ★ ★

Out of all the prisoners besides Bronka, Tchechia enjoyed talking to *Kapo* Benjamin Rakowski the best. They did not work together but would sometimes stand next to each other in the supper line. After a few days of talking to each other in line, they began to wait for each other, and whoever got there first would linger and not join the line until the other arrived. Tchechia enjoyed Benjamin's sense of humor. Even though they did not have the same kind of upbringing, Rakowski told stories in such a way as to make Tchechia laugh.

Tchechia was the daughter of a wealthy industrialist from southern Poland. She had a good education and considered becoming a nurse before a future career became impossible for Jews. Her parents were respected well by the business community and Tchechia was commended as being highly intelligent by many of her teachers. A rising star, they said.

However, her sharp wit would occasionally land her in trouble. Sometimes Tchechia spoke before she thought of the impact of her words. Her friends would sometimes call her "wild child" and Tchechia thought it was because of her flowing reddish-blond hair; later she considered that it might be because she could not keep her mouth shut.

It was hard for her to put her finger on what drew her to *Kapo* Rakowski. He was not very attractive, though he did have an athletic build. He looked strong and healthy, which was partially what set him apart from some of their camp-mates, who were emaciated. He made her laugh. That was the bottom line. It was probably the main reason she enjoyed being around him. And finding humor in a place like Treblinka was very rare.

Tchechia had men pay attention to her before; even the SS guards at Treblinka seemed to hold their gaze on her longer than she thought they should. But many of the men in her hometown who wanted to court her seemed too stuffy and boring. Occasionally her father would introduce her to one of his plant employees, perhaps hoping that Tchechia would take an interest. But each time, Tchechia would end up saying something that would hurt the boy's feelings.

It was not that she would set out to intentionally hurt someone—it just happened. All would start out well... *Tchechia, let me get the door for you, Let me help you with your coat, Let me tell you something about myself...* Then Tchechia would get annoyed. So many of the boys she had gotten to know would get nervous around her and just talk about themselves, as if she was inclined to be interested in their lives.

It wasn't in her to be a nice little girl, sitting by her courter to admire him for who he was. She would rather go climb a tree together, or swing from the rafters and jump into a haystack from the second floor of a barn, or simply swim in a river. So Tchechia would say what was on her mind, like: *I really don't care*, or *Please don't tell me anything else*, or *You're boring me.* The boy would take immediate offense, get flustered, and excuse himself from her presence.

With *Kapo* Rakowski it was different. It was almost as if he assumed she would not be interested, and he had a sort of self-deprecating humor that she found humble and attractive. He would say things like, *You must be waiting here for somebody else. I can get him for you if you would like*, and it would make her smile. He seemed clever and at ease with himself, which made her feel at ease as well, even at a dreadful place like Treblinka. So they stood in line together and whispered things about their day, such as which SS guard they encountered, which SS guards were going away for two weeks of leave, or discuss which of their friends had either been killed or sent to Camp 2.

It was cold outside this winter day. Tchechia and Rakowski stood in line together and stomped their feet. The transports of Jews had slowed down and that was disconcerting to everyone. They all understood that when they were no longer considered needed, the Nazis would dispose of the workers...just as they did to all the other Jews who were unfortunate enough to travel there. The pair also discussed the growing typhus issue.

"Men have been succumbing to it more frequently and we can usually detect it because they grow very weak and irritable," Rakowski told Tchechia, who already knew about typhus from working with Dr. Chorazycki. "But Galewski said we should never to call it typhus. If the guards hear that, they will simply shoot whoever has it. We have been calling it *Treblinka*, as a nickname. You can't catch it from someone else; it is spread by lice."

"I despise the lice," Tchechia said. "We can never get rid of them and it makes sleeping so uncomfortable."

"You don't like swatting lice all night?" Rakowski asked with a smile. "It is an adventure for me! I have names for them."

Besides survival, Benjamin Rakowski's daily goal in life was to try to get Tchechia to smile. But soon he turned the conversation more serious. "I hear the clinic is beginning to fill up with people who have *Treblinka*."

"Yes, it is filling up. All twenty beds are taken. Once it got cold outside, more and more people came down with *Treblinka*. Miete and Mentz make their rounds every day, looking for those the doctor says are too sick to recover. Then they take the poor soul to the *Lazarette*."

"It won't be much longer now," Rakowski said very quietly and stoically. "Zelo and Galewski have been planning, every night, more and more preparing and plotting."

"Hopefully it will be soon. Bronka is not looking well. I am afraid for her if she comes down with *Treblinka*. There are no beds. And the Angel of Death does not care if it is a man or woman who he takes out—it is all the same to him."

The two ate their soup and bread, drank their coffee, and were now ready to say goodbye. Tchechia would return to her quarters and Rakowski back to the male barracks.

"Don't get sick," Rakowski said.

"You, too. Otherwise I will not have someone to speak to in the mess line."

"How about Galewski?" Rakowski said with a grin. "He's older and more experienced with women. You might like his company."

"He *is* nice…just don't get sick," Tchechia said, smiling.

Rakowski pulled out a large chunk of ham from his coat pocket and handed it to Tchechia.

"Where did you get this?" she inquired, her eyes wide with astonishment.

"Don't ask," he replied, smirking. "Just enjoy it."

Tchechia knew that Rakowski was too daring when it came to trading valuables with other workers or the Ukrainians. She did not want him to get caught, or their budding friendship would be instantly severed. She slipped the ham into her pocket and departed from his company.

★ ★ ★ ★ ★   ★ ★ ★ ★ ★

The sun was deep behind the trees when the young people said their goodbyes. They could not discern that on the berm between the two camps there was a man in a white jacket, watching them speak. While standing there he tapped the top portion of his boots with the edge of his riding crop.

CHAPTER 13

One morning, several members of the Czech contingent stood amused. A boy holding an accordion was parked on the platform, off to the side. All they could see of him was his head and his feet—the accordion hiding the rest of his body. They soon learned he was fourteen years old and his name was Edek. He was selected by a Nazi guard out of his railcar to be used for entertainment, and he was bereft of his parents.

★ ★ ★ ★ ★   ★ ★ ★ ★ ★

Late in the evening, past lights-out, a shipment of two thousand Jews arrived on a train from Grodno, Belarus. The male barracks remained padlocked, but the Czech contingent could hear most of what transpired because of the proximity of their barracks with the rail platform. The SS guards—along with the help of the Ukrainians—decided to do all the work themselves and the unloading proceeded as normal until the passengers were told to undress.

Soon there were shouts heard through the group. "Do not undress! Resist! Do not listen to the Germans!"

Immediately there were gunshots and explosives heard. A few of the passengers were equipped with knives and pistols and tried to kill their German captors, all to no avail. Hand-to-hand combat using mostly sticks and fists was not very effective after the Germans set up a machine gun. Some of the Jews tried to escape the camp by fleeing to the high barbed-wire walls, only to be mowed down with rounds from the machine-gun fire, thus ending the crudely organized coup.

The next morning at roll call, Kiewe exploded in anger at everyone in his sight. After roll call, the Czech men were ordered to clean up the camp. What they saw was the devastating remains of a failed mutiny. Body parts littered the camp from the grenades and other explosives. A few men had to be peeled off the barbed wire. None of the valuables were organized, simply strewn about from one end of the camp to the other. It had been a late night for the Nazis, so they were in a worse mood than usual. A few had been injured, but sadly, the SS men who were living nightmares to the inmates—the Doll, Kiewe, Miete, and Mentz—were still alive and well.

Kurt Franz retained some of the rebels from the previous night to torture in front of the Jewish workers as a lesson if they should ever think about trying to revolt. He tied four men to wooden poles in the courtyard, left them—their bodies wounded—until midday, when he organized a camp formation. The Doll was in rare form: boots ultra-polished, uniform starched, a long bull whip held by his well-oiled deerskin gloved hand, and a mocking look on his ironically cherubic face.

The Doll relished every stroke with dramatic flair by running at his opponents, whip in hand, allowing them to feel the maximum bite out of every blow. He did not spare their faces or their genitalia. After thirty-five minutes, their mutilated corpses had stopped breathing. The Doll was depleted himself, sweaty and fatigued, exerting all his strength into the "lesson" for those in attendance. As a finale to his spectacle he dropped the bull whip, turned to the camp workers, and said, "You will encounter a similar fate if your mind becomes poisoned with betrayal and you try to escape. You will not succeed, but will die just as these men have died. This is very clear for you."

He then walked off, back toward the SS section of the camp and his quarters.

★ ★ ★ ★ ★   ★ ★ ★ ★ ★

In the quiet darkness of a cold and wintry night, seven men from Camp 2 tried to escape through a tunnel. Five had made it through to the other side of the camp wall when a Ukrainian guard shined a spotlight on them and opened fire. The two who were still in the tunnel crawled safely back into their barracks. Unfortunately for the ones who made it out of the tunnel, there was fresh snow on the ground and their footprints led the Nazi patrol right to the men. Of the five, one was shot on the spot. Three were brought back to the camp, where the Doll tortured them like a wild wolf at a feeding frenzy. They were hanged and left dangling for hours as additional discouragement. Only one made it out of the camp alive.

★ ★ ★ ★ ★   ★ ★ ★ ★ ★

Richard Glazar and David Brat stood on the rail platform, watching the new transports. They were to assist the blue bands by cleaning out the cars after the people had departed. As soon as the doors opened there were shouts and whips, exhorting people out of the trains. The two men watched as a man tried to navigate, exiting the train with two large packages in his arms. The woman behind him tripped on the head of a dead body and knocked into the man, causing one of his packages to fall and break open onto the platform.

When the man turned to bend over and help her up, he was beaten in the head by Kiewe's whip. Then his other package was knocked out of his arms. As a result, an older woman fell and more people tripped over her, tearing her skirt and exposing legs smeared with filth.

David whispered, "Richard, my boy, you Czech men don't know… none of you know. You arrived on passenger trains. For us Poles, Treblinka started in the ghettos. And almost everyone aids in some way to get rid of the Jews. Or at least they have in some way assented…"

Richard thought about what David told him. Perhaps he had lived a much easier life in Prague, where Jews were treated well and allowed to enter most career fields. He would ponder David's words some more when he had time to think about them.

The blue bands continued to do their work on the platform with the help of Kiewe, Miete, and the Doll. Afterward, the red bands shuttled the women through the large barracks building, where they were stripped, sheared, and sent into the tube. The men followed. By midmorning all of their trousers, dresses, blouses, shirts, coats, ties, hats, underwear, shoes, and socks were placed in neat piles. By midafternoon all of the valuables, including suitcases of hair, were bundled and packed onto the train.

This trainload did not have many of the highly sought-after items, such as gold, money, watches, and foodstuffs. It was composed mostly of Gypsies and other poor people from White Russia, a disappointment to Treblinka's workers.

It was in those final hours of December when the Czech men first saw the large, bright fires coming from Camp 2. As they looked out through a barred barracks window, the flames were visible over the top of the sandy berm that separated the two camps. In the stillness, Edek began to play a sad song on his accordion, "*Eli Eli*." With the music, and the memory of who was the fuel for the flames, everyone went to bed with deeper melancholy than usual.

CHAPTER 14

It was 1943.

More trains.

More shouting, more shooting.

More stench permeating the air from Camp 2.

The older passengers were carried on stretchers by blue bands to the *Lazarette*, where Mentz shot them in the neck, then pushed them into the flames inside the trench.

The Czech men worked at separating the clothing that was stuck together with sweat and dirt. They took two hundred shirts and put them on a large sheet and bundled them up. Shirts, shoes, pants, dresses, blouses, and underwear were all stacked into enormous piles in the courtyard.

Then one day, the trains stopped coming in. They had slowed down before but never stopped. This terrorized everyone.

★ ★ ★ ★ ★   ★ ★ ★ ★ ★

Franz Stangl had an announcement for all of the SS guards assigned to Treblinka.

"You have noticed...the trains to Treblinka slowing down...almost to a halt?" Stangl gently questioned. "For some reason Auschwitz was enhanced to accommodate an increase of transports, so we should expect a lull for a few weeks."

A brief silence filled the room as some of the Nazis considered the ramifications.

"What do you suggest we do with the workers until then?" inquired SS guard Otto Horn.

"I was hoping you would ask," answered Stangl with a grin. "We are going to do some construction work around here. I am authorizing, as of today, the construction of a remodeled railway station. I would like a tower with a large clock on it, a ticket office, and signs indicating which direction is Warsaw and Berlin—all just like a real station."

"But why?" asked Stangl's deputy Kurt Franz. "What's the point?"

"The point is the same strategy as to why we tell the passengers to keep their valuables, and that they are simply going to the showers after processing. That is the point," Stangl said in a deflated tone. He was forced to expound on his idea. "It will make things easier for us once they get off the trains. But that is not all. I want to change the area where we are living as well. We will have a main street, an entertainment area, and a park with some benches over by the woods. I want to make this place enjoyable for the staff, not just a malodorous drudgery."

"Why not a zoo?" mocked Franz with a grin.

"A zoo! Now there's a remarkable idea. And you will be just the man to coordinate getting the animals. It can be set up next to the park. We have the space, let's use it. Corporal Horn, I know there is a master builder in Camp 2, though I cannot remember his name. Please have him pick out a dozen men to assist him, then have him report to me tomorrow morning so I can explain to him what to do. We have some building supplies stored so he can get started right away, and I will also order more. What is the man's name?"

"Jankiel Wiernik," answered Horn.

"That's right. A delightful fellow. Send him over tomorrow and I will speak to him. Please don't fret about the lack of trains. It will take some time but we will get our construction finished and then be a solid camp for new shipments."

It was Kuttner who spoke up next. "What about the workers here in Camp 1? The piles are getting low. What do you suggest doing with them when there is no more work?"

"Well, we will have to cross that bridge when we come to it. Some of them will work with Wiernik to help with the construction, perhaps several dozens of them. I am told that eventually trains will begin coming again as they did last summer, perhaps more trains from the west. If the Allies ever land on the continent, the Fuhrer will probably move those in the western concentration camps to the east."

"What about the Russians?" asked Franz Suchomel.

Another moment of uneasiness.

The possibility of actually losing the war in the east was a dreaded thought upon which most of the men cared not to ever ponder.

Stangl chose his words thoughtfully and tried to sound confident. "It will take them at least a couple of years to recuperate before they try to regain their ground. We have hit them hard. Not hard enough, apparently, but hard. I still have hope. Stalingrad is a setback, not a failure. Be assured, we will prevail."

★ ★ ★ ★ ★   ★ ★ ★ ★ ★

Zelo Bloch held a meeting with his fellow conspirators. He had stationed guards at every window and two men near the door. Earlier in the day he met with Jankiel Wiernik. Being from Camp 2, Jankiel would be helpful relaying information back to those men committed to the revolt. The revolt became known as plan H. All the men understood the uprising would take the lives of many men and women, but for the chance to burn Treblinka to the ground and for hundreds of prisoners to escape, it was absolutely worth the risk for them to continue planning.

While the men listened to Zelo, it seemed he had conceptualized every single detail of the revolt day. "At the H hour we will have three men posted at each of the barracks' entrances," Zelo explained. "People can come in, but only messengers will leave. If any of the SS guards or Ukrainians enter they will quickly be put to death."

"How?" asked Hans.

"Once a guard enters, a coat will be placed over his head and then a cord will be used to strangle him. We do not want any loud noises like a gunshot—no blood, no struggle—because they will most likely keep coming in, one right after the other. We need them to *wonder* what's going on enough to enter, but not *suspect* any foul play yet."

"Where will we put them so they're not noticed?" Hans asked, again the curious one.

"That's easy," answered Robert. "We have the large piles against the back wall. We can put them in the hollow place where we hide workers who are sick with *Treblinka*. If the guard doesn't die right away, we can drag him to those piles and finish him off."

"That's right," continued Zelo. "If more than one guard comes in at the same time, we'll first attack the higher rank, then the second higher rank. The important thing is that once someone comes in, they do not leave under any circumstances. We will need plenty of men at each entrance ready to pounce and to guarantee there is no escape.

"After we kill the guards, we will use their weapons to commandeer the ammunitions stockpile, then set fire to the buildings. Several of us will have to storm the arms room together in case one of us is shot. It would also be good to have someone on the roof providing cover fire. Rudi, that would probably be a good job for you."

Rudi grinned. "I would like nothing better than to be on the roof with a machine gun. My only prayer will be that the Doll actually comes out into the open."

"There is a rumor that Stangl receives a call every hour from head-quarters; that is a concern. We will have to somehow mitigate this threat by cutting the phone lines, or perhaps taking out Stangl so he doesn't answer the phone. Camp elder Galewski said he would have men to deal with the phone wires. However, we need more information about what happens in the SS office."

Zelo continued, saying, "I will speak to both *Kapo* Rakowski and Dr. Chorazycki tomorrow to ensure they are ready to move forward and to see how the stockpile of money is coming. Another young Polish man, Samuel Willenberg, said he could be used to smuggle gold and banknotes from the gold team to the doctor."

Robert continued. "I spoke to the doctor today and he showed me a duffel bag practically bursting with gold. Thankfully the SS trust him and even ask him for medical advice regarding sick family members. If anyone has no need to worry about being dragged to the *Lazarette* by Miete, it is the doctor."

"What about those poor souls in Camp 2?" asked one of the non-Czech men in the meeting.

"Good point," replied Zelo. "They will know the date and hour ahead of time through Jankiel. However, they will only know when to start tak-ing action when they hear the explosions. As soon as we have set fire to the buildings in Camp 1 we will go to Camp 2 to help them, and then hopefully all escape together. My remaining concern is about the guard towers."

"I have a plan for that," continued Robert. "I spoke to Jankiel and some of the other carpenters coming over to work on Stangl's station. They all agree that on the day of the revolt they will need to have a prede-termined number of men to either climb the tower to take out the guard or somehow kill the guard while he is in the tower."

"Perhaps the Ukrainians there can be bribed," suggested Rudi. "Or if we get one of the watchtower guards to think a worker is bringing him gold, then the worker can climb up and kill him to subdue the machine gun—that would be a good way to do it. However, if there are already explosions at Camp 1, then the guards will all be on alert."

"Good idea, Rudi. Next, we have the chief mechanic, Standa Lichtblau, with us at the garage," continued Zelo. "Thankfully Standa said he could provide us with at least one hundred liters of gasoline, disbursed into several five-gallon cans, on the day of the revolt. This is what we will use to burn the buildings. He also said there is two to three times that amount in the main storage tank by the pump, and said that on the day of the revolt he could blow up the gasoline pump and storage container. This would be a massive explosion if accomplished. He will also disable all the vehicles the night before."

"The most important question," stated Robert, "is timing. We need to pick a day to get this done. I suggest two weeks from tonight."

"It's too soon," said Zelo. "We need more coordination with the men from Camp 2 and we have been given a great opportunity over the next few weeks to have the carpenters here working on the train station. Let's try for thirty days, give or take. In a week we will have more information and be able to set a date. I still need to understand the inner workings of the routine at headquarters, and we need to solidify our plans on disburs-ing arms from the arsenal. If we can accomplish those two things then we can set a date, a date with enough time to ensure Camp 2 people are on board and able to participate effectively."

Richard, Karel, and Hans listened attentively while Zelo, Rudi, and Robert explained all the details. It was obvious to all that Zelo was the catalyst and force behind all the planning, Robert was the scientist and the brains behind it, and Rudi had the military mind and brute strength to take bold action. Richard, Karel, and Hans recognized they, too, would have central roles to play on the big day, and that many of the prisoners were looking to the six Czechs for hope and guidance. The men knew that this would be their one great chance to escape—escape death, escape slaving every day for the Nazis in their pillaging of the passengers' valuables, and most importantly escape the death camp with their lives. The time of feigning obedience and loyalty to their tormentors was almost at an end.

★ ★ ★ ★ ★   ★ ★ ★ ★ ★

Days after the meeting concluded, men began dropping like flies with the fever of typhus. Twelve men reported to sick call in one day. The next day sixteen men awoke with a fever. The small Jewish sick bay remained overcrowded with deathly ill patients. Zelo became the first in the Czech contingent to get sick with a strong fever.

It was during his time in the sick bay that exercise drills were established in the barracks. There was not as much work to do so the guards believed the prisoners needed to participate in exercises. With whips, they would run the workers around the courtyard, telling the men to keep up or else malingerers would be shot on the spot. Everyone worked hard to keep together; the men in the front would intentionally slow down so their poor brothers in the back did not appear to fall behind. Sometimes the Doll would show up and have the men do an extra round of exercises just for fun. Some of the men who had started to get the fever began to foam at the mouth, and this drove the Nazi guards to speed them up even more, diligently searching for weak prey to take out of the pack.

The sick bay was not exempt from wolves seeking to thin the herds. The worst part of the day for the sick was when Miete made his rounds, looking for those struggling to make it. His daily consults with the doctor were the most feared discussions in the camp. Sometimes Miete resorted to the smallest infraction in order to yank someone out of the infirmary. If they looked too ill or if the sick hadn't shaved that day, they were grounds for Miete to take the prisoner to the *Lazarette*—no discussion and no debate. Miete acted as judge, jury, and executioner—a very efficient process.

CHAPTER 15

While the sickness raged inside the male barracks, Tchechia and Bronka were hard at work, trying to maintain their own sanity. Bronka and Rudi worked together under SS guard Franz Suchomel, who was—in comparison—not as criminal and crazy as Miete or Kiewe. However, he was still a Nazi, a committed National Socialist and had participated in Hitler's Action T4 euthanasia program before Treblinka. In fact, Rudi heard that the T4 connection was why Suchomel, Stangl, and the Doll were chosen to work at Treblinka—they were known as good Nazis who could keep secrets.

Rudi liked Suchomel because of his origins; both were Bohemian and had served in the Czech army. Bronka felt Suchomel was just as evil as the other men because he was complicit in all their actions. One day she argued with Rudi about this.

"If he is actually tenderhearted, then why doesn't he leave this place since he knows what is happening in Camp 2?" Bronka asked.

Rudi continued mending a jacket where he had just removed a Star of David while he answered, "I don't think he is allowed to leave. Once Globocnik assigns you somewhere you have to stay there. It is a police state now and everything that Hitler and Himmler say is the law."

"That is not true," Bronka countered. "Remember the one guard who left because he said he could not take this anymore?"

"Yes, but he was headed from here to the front lines. That is suicide."

"But in war he has a chance at being a decent man, in dying a decent death. Here, there is no option. By working here Suchomel does not have a chance at being a decent man. It does not matter whether the Germans win or lose, he will not have an honorable record. I think his chances in war would be better. If he becomes a casualty here there is no hope for him."

Rudi looked at Bronka somewhat seriously with her remark about dying at Treblinka. Any inference to the revolt was strictly forbidden outside of Zelo's planning meetings, or speaking directly with Zelo. Rudi was conscious that sometimes others were secretly listening in on conversations. He was not sure that this was what Bronka meant, but it could easily be taken the wrong way.

Bronka acknowledged Rudi's look of concern, then continued. "Please, Rudi, tell me you see my point. Say you understand what I mean about his life choices."

"I agree with you…in the central part. However, compared to Miete or Kiewe, Suchomel is a saint. He does not strive to murder people every day, nor weed out the undesirables. The Doll could walk into this room at any minute and send us to the *Lazarette*. I do not fear that with Suchomel," explained Rudi. "He is complicit in the evil, no doubt, but not a murderer."

"He may not be a sadist like the devils you just named but he is evil, and he does kill people."

"I have not seen him deliberately kill someone. Besides, isn't Suchomel the guard who chose you to be a seamstress? Didn't he save your life?"

Though Suchomel had saved Bronka from going into the tube, and he had been pleasant on the outside, her heart grew cold just being around him. He would attempt to get personal and discuss items with Bronka as if they were on the outside and did not have a prisoner-guard relationship. But it never satisfied Bronka. To her he was overly pleasant, or trying too hard, and she knew the ugly truth about his life that he could never camouflage. She knew what he was capable of doing, so it did not matter how nice he was to her. Bronka could see through him, and his smile that masqueraded the truth.

"Rudi, two weeks ago in the sorting barn I watched a little girl in her mother's arms while they were waiting for the barbers. Suchomel walked up to the girl and tried to take a doll out of the girl's hand, but the little girl refused and held tighter. Suchomel pulled out his pistol and shot the mother, right there, while she was holding her child. Then he grabbed the doll out of the distraught girl's arm and walked out of the building. And you say to me he is not evil? How can you say this thing to me? I have also seen him move women toward the barbers, telling them to hurry up because the water is getting cold. He is a liar, and he is evil. The fact that he can remain here, knowing what is going on and participating in these crimes, tells me this, and I do not need your agreement. I know what I know, and I saw what I saw."

Bronka had gotten herself worked up. It was not like her to express her feelings to anyone at the camp besides Tchechia. But she believed she could confide in Rudi with her inner feelings. He was not like the others. He had a soft face and warm heart, and she knew that with men like him planning the revolt, it might truly work. She felt she could trust him, and she shared one last detail. "Shortly after the shooting, Suchomel brought me the doll so I could sew a new dress for it."

Rudi looked at Bronka who had moist eyes while she spoke of the mother and the daughter. He admired her. She knew what she believed and she would not back down. Rudi thought about the doll dress and the shooting of the girl's mother. Bronka was rightfully upset in the midst of such horror, but with people dying all around them, he had not personally been alarmed about Suchomel. But now he saw her point.

Rudi responded tenderly, "Bronka, you are right. Please forgive my words. I should not have tried to give a defense for Suchomel's behavior. I agree with everything you have told me. I guess in my thankfulness to be alive and not worry about death during the hours I am working in this shop, I have overvalued the man's decency. And I do think it would be more honorable for him to outright quit, or desert, or transfer, than to be party to what Stangl and his henchmen are doing here."

"Or even suicide," she added.

Bronka deeply appreciated Rudi's words to her because she could tell that he was being sincere. This conversation helped her. Now Rudi understood how she felt. Now Rudi would know what Bronka was thinking and feeling whenever he might speak to Suchomel in her presence. It felt good to know that at least one other person in the camp knew how she felt about the Nazis and being at Treblinka. She did not know what the future held for her. She occasionally heard rumors about the revolt from Tchechia, and she frequently fantasized about how she might escape the camp, but a deeper thought always seemed to haunt her as she tossed and turned on her hard bunk at night—that she would probably die there. Swatting the lice on her legs, she contemplated that one day she might end up in the *Lazarette* with all the other poor souls.

"Thank you, Rudi. I liked your words." Bronka flashed a slight smile to show her appreciation. Then she went back to work.

★ ★ ★ ★ ★   ★ ★ ★ ★ ★

Tchechia stood by the much taller *Kapo* Rakowski in the darkness just after receiving their rations for the nightly chow. They knew they only had a moment to speak. Rakowski took a biscuit out of his pocket and handed it to Tchechia.

"Benjamin, it is too dangerous for you to do these things for me," said Tchechia, trying to sound mad but overjoyed at the small yet appreciated gift. "Someone could be watching us."

"I couldn't help myself," said the smiling *Kapo*. "I asked Frau Blau for it and she gave it to me."

"You shouldn't have! What if she tells her husband? You know the man is friends with *Kommandant* Stangl?"

"She won't tell him. She likes me. Anyway, just enjoy it."

"They are husband and wife! She probably tells him everything. We better part," declared Tchechia.

"Just half a minute more!"

"Why?"

"Because who knows what tomorrow might bring?"

"And what do you mean by that?"

"Well, I spoke to camp elder Galewski today."

"And?"

"And he was searching for information to help Zelo with plan H."

"When is it going to be?"

"I don't know, but I think it will be soon. Just stay safe until then."

"I'll try. Goodbye, *Kapo* Rakowski."

"Goodbye, Tchechia."

CHAPTER 16

Z elo Bloch's severe case of typhus finally turned its course and he was released from the sick bay. But as soon as he rejoined his comrades, Robert fell victim to the flu and was admitted to the care of Dr. Chorazycki. It was maddening for the conspirators because it would again delay their planning. It seemed as if the day for the revolt kept getting pushed back for one reason or another.

Zelo told his friends of a gift he had secretly received from Suchomel via Dr. Chorazycki: an unrotten orange with a soft peel. Suchomel also delivered a cup of soup to him from the German mess. Rudi thought of his conversation with Bronka and knew the other SS guards would have never acted with such kindness. However, her points were still valid.

Even though Robert would be in the sick bay for a while, Zelo was ready to start planning again in earnest with the rest of them, and he was anxious to find out what preparations the group had made in his absence. As soon as the Czech men began to update Zelo, there was a whistle from someone on lookout.

In a flash, Kiewe flew into the barracks with a whip in hand and a face red with fury. He was dressed in a dark-green uniform and there was drool visible in one corner of his mouth. For some reason he suspected wrongdoing. He ordered the men to count the bundles of shirts that still remained at Treblinka. He had a hand receipt from Zelo, the foreman, which stated there should be 205 bundles of shirts, packed ten to a bundle.

"You have reported 205 bundles, Mr. Foreman, so 205 bundles there better be!" Kiewe said mockingly.

When the men who were sent to count returned, they reported only 132 bundles of men's shirts were present.

"Did you count twice?" asked Kiewe.

An affirmative reply.

Staff Sergeant Kuttner clicked his heels and said, "The two supervisors from Barracks A, forward."

Zelo and a fellow supervisor named Adasch came to the front. The other men froze. Richard, Hans, Rudi, and Karel stood erect, hands at their side, wondering what was about to happen. *Would this be the time to take action and start the revolt?* They would wait and follow Zelo's lead.

Zelo and Adasch stood resolutely in front of a scorning Kuttner.

"You already knew, didn't you?" Kiewe asked. "I can tell by your faces that you two foremen are the guilty parties here. I should shoot both of you right now." Kiewe looked over the heads of men to Galewski, who was standing near the back of the group. "Camp elder, come forward."

Galewski walked through the nervous bodies to stand before Kuttner.

"Camp elder, remove the supervisor armbands from these men. They will no longer be supervisors. In fact, as punishment, they will be sent to Camp 2 as common laborers. Once your armbands are removed, I want you two men to grab your bedrolls. I will be escorting you to Camp 2."

While Sergeant Kuttner issued his orders, Kurt Franz walked into the barracks and shouted, "What is all this chaos? What is going on?"

Kiewe shouted, "Camp 1, attention! We have a discrepancy in their reports, Camp Deputy. They have been lying about how many shirt bundles they have. They are short seventy-three bundles of men's shirts. I knew they were not being honest and I am making amends for this."

The Doll and Kiewe decided to make up for the short bundles by having all the men to strip off their shirts and place them in bundles of ten.

"If I see one man here wearing a shirt, he will be shot," Kiewe raged while flashing his whip. "There are 734 men here, so there will be 734 shirts on this pile—immediately!"

Once all the shirts were on the floor, bundles were created and stacked against the wall.

"Now you have 205 bundles," asserted Kiewe before he left. "And I better not see a shirt on any one of you until the next train comes in."

All of the now half-dressed men opened a path for the Doll and Kiewe, who were escorting Zelo and Adasch out of the barracks up to Camp 2. Those remaining knew that they would probably never see them again.

They are going to the death camp over a few missing lice-infested shirts? Richard wondered. *Zelo will be dead to us. The uprising plan is over. Without Zelo there will be no leadership!* Hopelessness set in faster than darkness flooding a room when a candle is snuffed, and their faces could not hide the despair.

Richard decided to make his way over to the sick bay to inform Robert. While all the Czech men had formed tight friendships with each other, Robert and Zelo were especially close. Zelo would make great plans, and then Robert—the theorist—would explain scientifically why they had to work. Now Robert was sick, and Richard needed to deliver some devastating news to him.

Richard walked through the sick room and found the bunks holding Robert. He climbed up and knelt down besides his friend. "They've taken Zelo to Camp 2, Robert. Zelo has left us." Richard could smell the fever on Robert. After explaining what happened, Richard descended from the bunk, leaving Robert quietly weeping at the news.

That evening, as the men were settling into their bunks and a contemplative stillness filled the room, Hans spoke the words bound up in everyone's heart. "It serves us right! We kept waiting and discussing. Each one of us is man enough to do what needs to be done; we could've made heads roll, but instead we just stood there, like sheep. They've gotten to us. Their work is complete. We aren't human beings anymore. I can't even believe in myself."

No one else said anything and Hans continued speaking out loud. "All I keep thinking about is my wife and curly haired son. You know, when he was a baby he had such delicate little cheeks, so soft, like the skin on his bottom. We stood there and waved at each other that first day, and do you know what I was thinking? I was hoping he would not catch a cold. A cold!

"That first day and night after I heard what happened to them, I didn't feel anything. It didn't register. I just ran back and forth with bundles on my shoulders. But a few days later it hit. My chest and throat and brain were burning. It was like I was filled with acid. All I wanted to do was to tear down everything, like that long-haired man they told us about in religion class who pushed over the pillars. Then I knew I was going crazy. Pull it together, I told myself. But you know what? Now they've gotten to us all, even the Ukrainians. What good is reason here? What we need is one of the mad long-haired men who tore down the pillars and brought everything crashing to the ground."

None of the Czech men said anything after that. Rudi thought about his own wife and the last time he saw her on the unloading platform. Richard and Karel were unmarried, but they thought about their parents and siblings. Karel knew his family's fate since they had arrived with him at Treblinka, but Richard still had no idea, though he assumed they were probably gone.

Everyone thought of Zelo, wondering how long he would last at Camp 2. They guessed the survival rate was much worse there because prisoners from Camp 1 were constantly being recruited to replace workers at Camp 2. It had to have a high mortality rate. They knew that Camp 2 was a true work camp, where every day men worked hard with little time to rest. Zelo would have to survive, and they would have to execute the revolt plan without his leadership.

★ ★ ★ ★ ★   ★ ★ ★ ★ ★

Robert was released from the sick bay and sent back to Barracks A. He was then given a complete report of what happened with Zelo and an update on the revolt plan. Rudi had taken over the leadership of the military operation, but he was wary of whom he could trust. The Jewish workers were always eyeing each other in order to identify those who might have sided with the Nazis. Despite the efforts of the *kapos* to weed out the bad eggs, there were still several informers among the men in Barracks A, and routinely they had to be "taken out" by creative means.

Thankfully Dr. Chorazycki was one of the most dependable, diehard conspirators in the camp. When an informer was brought to him, he knew exactly what to do to put the person out of his misery permanently, and without bringing any attention to the SS.

An additional incident hampered Rudi's planning shortly after he took his position as lead revolt planner: camp elder Galewski caught a severe case of typhus. Galewski was smart, straightforward, and one hundred percent trustworthy. The Nazis needed an acting camp elder and the Doll replaced Galewski with the much younger *Kapo* Rakowski, someone with whom Rudi was not familiar because they had not spent much time together.

Rakowski was very different than Galewski, not only in age, but in experience, people skills, work ethic, tact, and diplomacy. Trading goods and making bribes with the Ukrainian police was called speculating, and Rakowski was the largest speculator in the camp. He was constantly bargaining for hams and other foodstuffs, not only to share them with Tchechia, but to barter the items with the other Jewish workers. Speculators always walked a fine line with the Ukrainians because the guards could take the merchandise by force, without paying. Or worse, they could report the scheming worker to the SS guards. The Ukrainians were not honest brokers.

Speculator Rakowski, in essence, was now in charge of the camp, and Rudi was trying to ascertain how much planning he should do with Rakowski, knowing that at any moment he could be caught and tortured for speculating. *Who knows what kind of information Rakowski would reveal to the Nazis under torture?*

Things did not feel quite right in the camp, and to make matters worse, the trains had ceased coming altogether, not even a trickle. This weighed heavily on everyone. Without work to do, the Jews knew they were not useful to the SS and could be exterminated in the gassing chambers any day.

The Czech contingent eventually received an update on Zelo through carpenter Jankiel Wiernik. Their leader was surviving, and more interested than ever to get the revolt planned. Zelo now had a group of conspirators in the upper camp with whom he began meeting, but the uprising must be planned and executed initially from Camp 1, and Rudi was acutely aware of this.

★ ★ ★ ★ ★   ★ ★ ★ ★ ★

Things were getting desperate. On top of the lack of work due to the cessation of transports, the inmates were forced to drink the gruel from the camp provisions, something they despised and would work around at all costs. It was now a necessity; people were starving and it was the only nourishment afforded to them.

All of the confiscated items still lying around in piles were packaged and shipped out. The large mountains of eyeglasses and shoes were cleaned up and removed. There was no more clothing, no more pots and pans. Everything had been sent out. Rudi and Bronka had no more fabric stars to remove. The only work available to them was if a Nazi wanted a coat tailored. They all knew that life could not be sustained on the meager rations. There was near panic in the camp.

Just when they all feared Treblinka would close and gassing was inevitable, trains from Bulgaria arrived. The Nazis found out the night before. Stangl received a phone call to be prepared to receive thousands of Jews from the Balkans. The Doll decided to relay the news to the Jewish workers. He slipped into the barracks unannounced and told Rakowski in front of everyone the trains were going to be coming again starting the following day.

"Hurrah, hurrah!" the men screamed. It was not lost on them that it meant certain destruction for those being transported, but it signaled that they would get to live another few days. Death for others meant life for them. It was quite a relief.

★ ★ ★ ★ ★   ★ ★ ★ ★ ★

For the next few days, the Jewish workers processed men, women, and children from Bulgaria totaling twenty-four thousand. Especially gratifying was that the Bulgarians came from surplus, and not from the Warsaw ghetto. There were train cars full of supplies: enormous cheese rounds, crates of jam, tea cookies, and large packages of meat. The Jewish workers would accidentally drop a crate here and there to plunder the provisions from the Ukrainian guards patrolling the operations. When the crates broke open, food poured out onto the ground. They happily endured the whips for one large mouthful of fresh food.

The Bulgarians themselves were heavy people, with dark hair and dark eyes. They could have easily resisted the guards on the platform if they had the slightest suspicion that Treblinka was not a work farm. They dutifully undressed and carried their clothes over to the proper piles. Then they waited in line inside the tube, which led to the mock shower room.

Occasionally an arriving Jew would ask one of the Jews with red bands in the sorting barracks, "Keep an eye on my stuff for me, will you?"

The reply was always a nod, not with a smile, but with an attempt at assurance. In a few days all twenty-four thousand had perished, their clothes and other valuables separated in large mounds in the sorting yard—pyramids of remembrance to be crudely bundled and shipped out by the grateful souls still alive in the camp.

During their momentary abundance, Hans became ill-tempered at some of the Polish Jews for enjoying their current feast. They were eating containers of fish, cookies with plum butter on them, cornbread covered with cheese, and biscuits with jam.

"Good grief!" exclaimed Hans. "What is the matter with you people? Can't you stop and take a breath?" He yelled at two men who had continued to feast in their bunks after lights-out while others tried to rest.

"What's it to you, Hans?" they replied in Polish. "Why do you care?"

"I do care. Because you two have been stuffing your faces and giggling like girls all night. I can no longer stand the sight of you."

"Remember, we're in Treblinka, so how about some consideration?" the Polish men responded.

"Who cares?" bellowed Hans. "We're all in Treblinka. You don't see the rest of us acting like animals!"

"Who cares?" The men mocked Hans. "Look, boys, we have someone of importance here. A cultured Czech Jew. He doesn't act like an animal. It's amazing he ever ended up in Treblinka!"

At this point the anger in Hans boiled over. "I hate you all! Do you hear me? I hate every one of you disgusting Poles!" Hans took the whip he used as a section leader ever since Zelo departed and began to crack it into the darkness beyond his bunk. "The Doll is right: you like to wallow in your own crap!"

The Polish men were not bettered. "You German dupe! Jew hater! You're no better than a Nazi!"

Robert moved over to Hans and stuck a thermometer in him. It was as he suspected—Hans was burning with a fever.

CHAPTER 17

Tchechia was given a red armband and tasked with helping in the large wooden barracks to process the thousands of women and children that week. There was a flurry of activity and Tchechia went from person to person, assisting with their buttons and helping them with their socks. She did not yell at the new arrivals like the *kapos*; Tchechia spoke softly and assuredly to the bewildered travelers. Several of them asked why she wore the band, because her looks were so obviously not someone of Jewish origin. Tchechia always smiled in appreciation but reaffirmed that she was a Jewess, just like them.

Tchechia especially loved the children she helped. As much as the Nazis were rife with a coldness toward the youngest Jews, Tchechia was filled with compassion. The children looked to her for guidance to get through the ordeal. Many mothers had their hands full helping all of their little ones undress and remain calm, not to mention getting undressed themselves, then putting all of their garments into the correct piles. Tchechia noticed how the children looked at their mothers in wonder, watching them undress in front of all the other people. Tchechia tried to reassure everyone to continue to move so the guards would not get upset. She told them it was better to comply and leave the clothing behind than it was to argue and resist.

Though it seemed like years since she had seen her father and mother, and almost like an alternative life, Tchechia reflected it was not that long ago when she was happily in their company. She recalled their love for her, and for each other. She remembered her father constantly reminding her of how strong she was, yet she did not feel strong now.

At the time, it was not hard for Tchechia to say goodbye, something she currently felt guilty about because now she missed them fiercely. She wondered if they were still alive, or if Belzec was a camp like this one. She knew that her parents would not be pulled out of line for their youth and strength—they were middle-aged and looked like all the other people who ended up in the tube. She did not hear much about the other camps except one called Auschwitz. Word had gotten out that many Jews were sent right to the gas chambers there. She was thankful her parents were not sent to Treblinka or to Auschwitz, but she had no idea what kind of camp Belzec was.

Out of the corner of her eye, Tchechia noticed an older woman, still fully clothed and sitting on a pile of shoes. She would soon be beaten if Tchechia did not help her. She made her way through multiple naked bodies of women and children, several of whom were screaming. Before she arrived at the older woman a young boy grabbed Tchechia's hand.

"I'm so thirsty," the boy said to Tchechia.

Tchechia stopped, looked into his dark eyes, and knew he would never have another drink. She could not lie to him. She would not. The guards often told the new arrivals that they could drink in the showers and their thirst would be quenched, but their phony gesture was only meant to amuse themselves. Tchechia could not deceive others this way. That kind of humor was not funny to her.

Keeping the older woman in her peripheral vision, Tchechia knelt down beside the boy, straightened his tousled bangs with her thumb, and grabbed his cold hand before saying, "You know, when I'm thirsty, I usually try to think of something else to keep me from thinking about how thirsty I am."

"Like what?" the boy asked.

"Well, like what happened on my last birthday."

The boy thought for a moment, then looked mournfully at Tchechia and said, "I'm still thirsty."

Tchechia smiled at him, patted him on the head, and asked him what his name was.

"Jakub," the little boy responded. "What is yours?"

"You have a nice name, Jakub. My name is Tchechia. Is that your mom standing there?" Tchechia asked him while pointing to a woman nearby.

"Yes, and she is not happy right now."

"Well, would you please go stand by her? It looks like she is looking for you."

Gently guiding him toward his mother, Tchechia then walked quickly over to the older woman.

"Ma'am, can I help you with your clothing?" Tchechia asked as she knelt down and began removing one of the woman's shoes.

"You may, but I don't see the point," the woman responded.

"Why do you say that?" Tchechia asked. Still she would not lie to her and say she needed to be naked before she entered the shower.

"Because I suspect we are not really going into the showers, so there is no point for me to undress."

"Ma'am, it is not for me to say what will or will not happen to you, because I am not in charge of this camp. All I can say is that if we don't get you undressed right away a guard will come over here and start to beat you without mercy."

"But what does it matter?" the woman said, almost shouting.

There was so much commotion around them that no one noticed her raised voice, but Tchechia wondered if the woman would be shot right there in the undressing barracks, as she had seen happen before. She decided to try again.

"Ma'am, up now, get up," Tchechia said, forcefully grabbing the woman's hand and raising her up off the shoes. Then Tchechia began unbuttoning the woman's dress while the woman stared at her. The last button was unfastened near the woman's neck and Tchechia tried to slip the dress off, but the woman turned away from her, making it impossible.

At this point the people around them were forming into lines, waiting to be sheared. Almost everyone was undressed except for a few children who were being helped by their mothers. Tchechia knew it was a matter of seconds before the woman would be targeted as a noncompliant by someone in charge.

She stared at the woman. The woman stared back. Tchechia reflected she might have had the same attitude if the roles were reversed, though she herself had undressed immediately, thinking this was a real work camp.

Months had passed since then. News about Treblinka had no doubt disseminated throughout Poland. When the passengers saw the station sign, some of them had to know that this was the end, like the woman standing before her.

A *kapo* was heading right for them. Tchechia did not want to see this woman's blood shed around her. In a final desperate attempt, Tchechia lunged at the woman, grabbed her dress, and ripped it off her arms. It was too easy. The woman must have complied. With the removal of her under-wear she was naked and standing in line with everyone else. She never stopped staring at Tchechia...and Tchechia could not forget her woeful eyes, devoid of hope.

The *kapo* found another person to harass.

Tchechia walked out of the building, haunted by the look in the old woman's eyes.

★ ★ ★ ★ ★   ★ ★ ★ ★ ★

Treblinka had changed. The new mock train station was finalized, complete with a fake clock on the side of the tower where the hands were permanently painted on the outer wall. The eternal time was six o'clock. A new fence for the zoo had been set up and animals were starting to arrive. *Kapo* Rakowski, knowing there would soon be an uprising and that Jews would have to flee into the woods, thought he should march the Jewish workers around to the music. This would build up their strength and endurance to escape the patrols that would certainly be sent to capture them immediately after the revolt. The Doll agreed to this exercise and cheered them on. It formed into an evening parade after roll call.

The weather began to turn warmer and the sun was setting later and later. Though few transports were arriving, and some nearly empty—like the one in which over three-quarters of the passengers were already corpses—the Nazis and the Jews were being creative in occupying their time. There was a new camp "street" with an elaborate, country-style gate by the rail station, benches, flowers, and buildings painted with bright col-ors. There was the continuous sound of construction in the camp as it was reshaped, all to specifications of *Kommandant* Stangl and the Doll. Usually the arrival of spring brings new hope, but for the revolt organizers this was when disaster struck.

CHAPTER 18

One day in April, Kurt Franz walked into the German sick bay to see Dr. Chorazycki. After the usual pleasantries, Franz was about to tell the doctor the reason for his visit when he noticed there was a bulging handbag in the corner of the office. Franz asked the doctor what was in the bag, and then stepped over toward it. As the Doll was investigating the bag, stuffed with 150,000 zloty and other valuables, Dr. Chorazycki quickly grabbed a surgical knife and lunged at the deputy *kommandant*, stabbing him in the back.

"What the...? You stinking Jew!" cried Franz. "Do you think you are going to get away?"

Regrettably for the doctor, it was a small knife plunged into a large back. The Doll shouted out for a couple of comrades as the fifty-seven-year-old doctor fled the clinic. During the time of his escape and subsequent capture, Chorazycki had time to swallow some poison. Unfortunately it was not enough.

When the SS guards finally caught the former Warsaw doctor, they began to kick and beat him mercilessly. The Doll arrived and also joined in, but Chorazycki had passed out. The guards carried the bloody frame over to the courtyard, where the Doll had earlier installed a whipping post as part of the camp *enhancements*. An irregular roll call was set for mid-afternoon so that everyone could see what happened to traitors. At the formation, Deputy Franz walked up, newly bandaged and wearing a clean uniform.

"Do you see what happens when you are crazy enough to attack one of us?" the Doll challenged. He then had the guards pour a couple of buckets of cold water on Chorazycki's body. The body twitched, giving the Doll the assurance he needed that there was life underneath the shredded clothing, dirt, and blood. Franz went to work, looking into the eyes of his audience after every lash. Through the first fifteen strikes there was some movement when the blows landed, but after a terminal exhale, there was nothing. This did not deter the Doll, however, who continued to strike the lifeless body. Twenty, thirty, forty…fifty total lashes.

"Now drag him to the *Lazarette* to be shot!" Franz demanded. Then the Doll stared at the assembly of workers before him. "This Jew swine had gold and zloty and dollars in his possession. And I know he got it from somewhere. Therefore I want all the gold Jews to follow me to the *Lazarette* because I am going to get to the bottom of this treachery."

Although already very dead, Dr. Chorazycki was shot for good measure, then thrown into the perpetual flames of the death trench. The Doll turned to the Jewish workers who worked with the gold assembled before him. Edek, the young accordion player, was also forced to be there. The boy was crying, begging the others to tell what they knew because he didn't want to die.

Each Jewish worker was individually brought up to face the edge of the pit. Franz put his handgun in each man's back and demanded, "Now tell me what you know. Where did the doctor get the money? Tell me, or I am going to shoot you. If you do tell me, you will live." One by one the gold Jews marched up to Franz, who handled them roughly and then let them go. For some reason, even though no information was revealed, only the doctor was killed that afternoon. Franz knew that Stangl would be upset if he followed through with his executions. The gold Jews were too important to take out of commission en masse. Standing together in secrecy, they all retained their lives.

★ ★ ★ ★ ★   ★ ★ ★ ★ ★

A few weeks after the death of Dr. Chorazycki, the SS decided to perform another random inspection to see if anyone else was stashing gold or dollars. A Nazi staff sergeant bellowed to the assembly of workers, "Anyone found with money in his possession, even as small as a penny, will be severely punished."

The search in Barracks A progressed smoothly until they searched acting camp elder Benjamin Rakowski's bedroll, where there was stored a large amount of gold, money, and other valuables. It was almost as if they knew before they searched that they would find a cache of goods.

The Nazis laid out all of the newly discovered items in front of the formation. Then Miete asked for Rakowski and Galewski, who had not been formally reinstated following his typhus recovery, to come forward.

Miete roughly removed Rakowski's armband. "You are no longer the camp elder." He then told Galewski, "You again are the Treblinka camp elder for the workers." He motioned for Galewski to return to the formation, then looked at Rakowski. "*Kapo* Rakowski, these items were found in your possession. What do you have to say for yourself?"

Before he allowed Rakowski to answer, Miete pulled out his pistol and stuck it in Rakowski's back. "March!" Miete ordered.

"Wait a minute!" shrieked Rakowski, realizing the end had come. He stopped walking, forcing Miete to yank him toward the door.

"Wait a minute!" the former camp elder yelled. The face of Tchechia flashed in his mind and how disappointed she would be.

"Why?" barked Miete. "What do you have to say?"

"What I have to say is…these items are not mine," stammered Rakowski, trying to mask his terrific fear.

"Then whose are they?" asked Miete, always interested to uncover a worker plot.

"I have been set up by someone, by a traitor," suggested Rakowski.

"Who?" bellowed Miete.

At this point all the other men in the barracks held their breath. What would Rakowski say? Would he expose the revolt committee? Would the uprising have to start now?

"By Chorazycki!" shouted Rakowski. "The doctor hid those items in my bedroll, hoping to get me in trouble."

"Chorazycki's dead," replied Miete.

"I know that. He hid them before he was caught. He stored items all over."

Miete eyed him suspiciously. "If you knew he was hiding stolen items, then why didn't you report it? Huh, if you are so faithful? Why would you never tell me this information until now, when you are caught red-handed?"

"I couldn't," said Rakowski as convincingly as possible.

"Why not?"

"Because Chorazycki threatened my life!"

"But now he is dead and you are no longer threatened, yet you did not come to us. Let's go!" Miete knew that it was a typical tactic of the Jewish workers to blame someone who had already been killed, then there could be no reprisals. Miete was convinced Rakowski was guilty and he wanted to make an example out of him. Putting to death the acting camp elder would implant fear in all of them, showing that no one was above the law.

Miete marched Rakowski over to the *Lazarette* where Sergeant Mentz was waiting. The Jewish workers heard a single shot, and then Miete walked out of the *Lazarette* alone.

Later that evening, the Doll decided to take the opportunity to give the men a lecture. In it, he told them that Rakowski was executed because of extortion, speculation, and for defrauding Greater Germany. It was an eloquent speech.

The Czech contingent whispered together about the setbacks during that night's planning meeting. They had lost their leader Zelo, Dr. Chorazycki, and now Rakowski, all within a short period of time. The SS guards were cracking down, and it felt as if they were closing in on the plans for the revolt. This influenced some of the men to quit active participation in the planning—but not the Czechs.

★ ★ ★ ★ ★   ★ ★ ★ ★ ★

Only Tchechia knew that Rakowski was storing the gold for their own personal escape. The two of them—unknown to anyone else—had planned to depart the camp the very evening *Kapo* Rakowski was executed. His sudden death was a shock but Tchechia did not cry. She knew that it would not help. Instead she decided to find another way to escape.

PART 3

CAMP 2

CHAPTER 19

When Zelo and Adasch first walked up to Camp 2, they both knew they were lucky to be alive…lucky they were not instead taken to the *Lazarette*. The first immediate impact to their senses was the stench. Though only a few meters from where they had lived before, the smell was more of an assault on their senses at their new quarters. They had witnessed plenty of misery in Camp 1, but in no way did it mentally prepare them for what they experienced in Camp 2.

They learned that there were two main gassing chambers. Each chamber possessed nickel-plated metal showerheads in the ceiling, and small orange terra-cotta tiles on the floor. During gassings, each chamber was crammed with 350–400 people at a time. Babies and small children were routinely tossed inside over the occupants' heads once it was too tight to fit any more adult-sized bodies. The doors tightly closed and a shout proclaimed, "Ivan, water!" A petrol-driven engine immediately started up, which sent carbon monoxide gas into the pipes that was released through the showerheads in each chamber.

The process to suffocate the unsuspecting Jews took roughly thirty to forty minutes. Then the order would be given to open the hermetically fitted iron doors facing Camp 2 so that the removal of bodies could begin. On days when the Nazi guards felt especially cruel they would delay the full treatment of gas in order to spread out the torture over six to twelve hours…then laugh about it.

When the guards could no longer hear any screaming, the extermination mission would be accomplished. "All asleep!" they shouted. The Jewish workers would then open the doors and the bodies closest to the door would fall out.

Immediately after his arrival, Zelo was introduced to the labor he

89

would perform for hours on end, every day—the processing of corpses. A large team of Jews spent their days hauling bodies from the gassing chambers to the large roaster racks to be burned. The Nazi mission at Camp 2 was to exterminate and dispose of the thousands of pitiful souls who had not been selected as Jewish workers at Camp 1.

Zelo was assigned to the transport squad. Once the gassing operation was cleared for removal the transporters ran everywhere. They ran to the large multichambered brick building. They hustled to extract the clammy corpses out of the rooms and place them outside. They loaded two adult bodies or three child-sized bodies onto a stretcher, and then ran toward the large burning pits. En route they would halt to allow amateur Jewish dentists extract teeth and thoroughly check all body cavities for gold, porcelain, and other precious substances. Then the men proceeded with their stretchers toward the grilling racks. A few weeks before Zelo arrived, the bodies were merely thrown into an enormous pit and covered with sand. But now, Camp 2 was following an order from Stangl to burn every corpse and dispose of the ashes.

★ ★ ★ ★ ★   ★ ★ ★ ★ ★

Zelo now understood the entire path of processing people through Treblinka. While still working in the lower camp, Zelo was tasked to chop pine branches in the woods. When the wagon was full, it was hauled up to the tube. The workers were instructed to carefully weave the branches throughout the fence to disguise the barrier.

Once, while peering through the tube, Zelo saw the processing of women and children being roughly herded down the channel. Ahead they could see a large Star of David and a dark ceremonial curtain, which declared in Hebrew, "This is the Gateway to God." Completely naked and with their arms raised, the passengers were kicked and hit with the butts of rifles while they clambered up five large concrete steps, through the doorway, and into the multichambered building.

Despite the obvious difference between the camp operations, Zelo realized there were some similarities. The men were locked in their barracks each night—morning roll call was held at 5:30 a.m. for strict accountability, there were *kapos* who helped supervise the upper-camp Jews, there were nearly a dozen women who worked at the upper camp as launderers and cooks, and there were guard towers with Ukrainians changing shifts several times a day. Everyone ran, everyone feared for their lives, and the German SS guards were sadists.

The stories Zelo heard those first few days from some of the other Camp 2 workers greatly troubled him. He became more determined than ever to continue planning for the uprising. He set about to rally the leaders of the upper camp with all of the information he possessed as a leader and former resident of Camp 1.

Soon after Zelo's arrival he became the lead conspirator of Camp 2. He possessed the rugged good looks and confidence of leadership and influence, a man who was at ease with himself and others. Friendly yet determined, his countenance suggested he would not take any dissonance or two-faced posturing from others. The guards, rather than taking offense to his chutzpah, approved of it, placing the mantle of leadership on Zelo by making him a *kapo* within the first month of his arrival.

Zelo knew he had to keep in communication with Camp 1 if the revolt was to remain unified and succeed. He became close friends with Jankiel Wiernik, the camp carpenter. Jankiel alone was trusted by the Nazis to go back and forth between the two camps because they needed his building expertise at the lower camp. He would speak to Rudi when working on his construction project at Camp 1, then report back to Zelo in the upper camp at night. In this way, the two camps stayed connected.

The work in Camp 2 was awful to endure. But Zelo's hope for retaliation and freedom inspired the Jewish workers there to keep laboring hard to stay alive.

CHAPTER 20

Because the transports had slowed down to a trickle, the Doll decided to get the people in Camp 1 working on additional improvement projects. The zoo, which now had foxes, squirrels, pigeons, peacocks, and other animals, continued to expand, so Jewish workers were tasked with constructing shelters for the new arrivals. The Doll also developed an orchestra, along with entertainment shows to be performed after evening formations, such as skits and boxing.

SS guards were all instructed by the deputy *kommandant* that while on vacation they should look to bring back as many instruments they could find. The camp also harvested many violins and brass instruments from the trains to use for the upcoming concerts. Soon an entire orchestra was formed from workers who were skilled musicians before their incarceration.

The Doll was notified that a famous Warsaw musician, Arthur Gold, had arrived on one of the transports. Franz immediately pulled the talented Jewish worker aside and told him about his exciting plans. Gold would be the conductor of the new Treblinka orchestra. The Doll had a podium built for the orchestra leader, and instructed him to work with the other musicians to compose a Treblinka hymn within two days.

But this was not the end to all of the Doll's plans. "From now on we will have a cabaret," he said to the Jewish workers at Camp 1. "Do not laugh, I am quite serious about this. We will have boxing matches, skits, singing…and I want to have a wedding. Yes, I will pick two people to get married, and then after the ceremony we will give them some alone time in the barracks. It will be called the wedding barracks!"

The Doll was quite pleased with himself with this announcement. It did not occur to him that in another time and place this might have been considered humorous. But in Treblinka, nothing could amuse the men and women who were in constant fear for their lives. Weddings, honeymoons, and sex were not on the minds of the workers. The austere conditions constantly reminded them that they were prisoners and not free to be entertained by shows and ceremonies. They each hoped to simply live one more day, thinking that perhaps something could alter their fate.

There continued to be no trains arriving at Treblinka. The cooks, tailors, carpenters, medical assistants, sorters, plumbers, maids, and goldsmiths did not have nearly enough to do. So work, in the form of amusement, was being laid before them.

★ ★ ★ ★ ★   ★ ★ ★ ★ ★

On the Sunday of the first concert, Camp *Kommandant* Stangl sat in the center of the front row, surrounded by the Doll, Kuttner Kiewe, Miete, Mentz, Suchomel, and the others. With orchestra conductor Arthur Gold at the front and little Edek at the back, the entire orchestra sat on camp chairs clutching their used instruments, each dressed in white jackets with blue lapels.

As Arthur Gold, a master violinist and composer, lifted his baton to begin the concert, a memory flashed in his mind of the magnificent Polish National Symphonic Orchestra that had assembled a few years before the war. With an international presence, Arthur Gold's compositions routinely played on radios across Europe. Now he was a prisoner inside Treblinka conducting an assemblage of prisoners, none of them playing their own instruments, and all of them afraid for their lives. In the air was the nauseating smell of roasting bodies, and concertina wire lined the perimeter of the square. With all the dignity Gold could muster, he flung out his arms and began the show.

The highlight of the concert were solos by the tenors—trained opera performers from Warsaw who were somehow recognized by fans when pulled off the trains and diverted away from the tube. The orchestra music itself was average, but considering it came forth from those with little time to practice together, it was remarkable. The Nazis knew that Gold had done well with the resources given him.

Following the concert was a boxing match between a large worker and small one for comedic effect. Then there was a reading of a newspaper with humorous stories given as asides. The final act was the wedding. As promised, the Doll picked out two of the younger Jewish workers and had them tie the knot. Thankfully Bronka and Tchechia were not chosen out of the few women available. Richard, Karel, Rudi, Hans, and Robert were similarly relieved. They did not want to participate in the Nazi ceremony, even if it was a sham.

The expression on the faces of the two workers chosen was of such disgust it drew the ire of some the SS in attendance. It was not much like a traditional wedding; no ceremonial expressions and no singing. Just a pronouncement and it was over. The two were sent off to the barracks to be alone. The Doll had accomplished his show for the day, and now the conclusion of the spectacle produced something else as well—pure terror in the hearts of all the workers. *What would they do next?*

CHAPTER 21

"We have to act now!" exclaimed Rudi Masarek. "Something is up. Something terrible. The time is now, either today or tomorrow. We have to take action."

It was a warm, late spring day, 1943. The Czechs were at their daily planning meeting for the revolt, led by Rudi. Several men were standing guard at the doors. The meeting was uncharacteristically taking place in the morning. The workers were instructed to remain in the barracks, which in itself was unsettling. The excuse the Nazis used was that there were no trains.

"Why the sudden rush, Rudi?" asked Richard.

"It is Galewski. One of the female workers told our camp elder that she overheard the Doll talking to Stangl. He said with the lack of trains, they did not need as many workers."

"This could be a setup," chimed in Robert. "They could be prodding us to see if we begin to act crazy."

"Regardless, they may choose to take two hundred of us to the *Lazarette* just for good measure. I think we are beginning to borrow time we do not have. I know we have the two pistols, but is there any news on the lock and the arms room?"

The revolt organizers had received two pistols and some ammunition from peasants who lived near the camp. The exchange took place in a clandestine manner; the peasant would discreetly hide packages for the Czechs at a distance, then held up two or three fingers if they wanted twenty or thirty dollars for them. In return, the money was hidden nearby at a later time.

Regarding the arsenal, it was surrounded by Ukrainians, but the lock had been "mysteriously" jammed. One day, little Edek, on orders from the revolt committee, dashed past the arms room and frantically shoved metal shavings into the lock when no one was looking. When it was discovered the lock did not work it immediately drew the suspicion of their Nazi overlords.

They commissioned the Jewish locksmith to remove the door to his shop where he was to repair the lock, but they did not trust him. Ukrainian guards supervised the locksmith so no additional keys could be made. However, the locksmith's entire family had disappeared down the tube at Treblinka, so he was sympathetic to the Czech men's plans.

Despite the watchful eye of the Ukrainians, the locksmith took an incredible risk by secretly making a wax impression of the key when the guards were distracted. From the impression, he was able to create an additional key. The Ukrainians were none the wiser. The locksmith gave one key to the SS, and one to the organizers for the revolt.

"Yes, we have the key," replied Karel. "We can have some of the young men, perhaps Edek and several others, break into the arsenal and steal the grenades."

"Do it," Rudi said stoically. "It is now or never. I will alert the upper camp; as soon as we have the grenades in our hands the revolt begins."

★ ★ ★ ★ ★   ★ ★ ★ ★ ★

That very day, little Edek and three of his friends nervously walked over to the guard's living quarters where the arms room was located. Their attempt at a nonchalant stroll was comical, but no one was around to notice as the guards were all on their rounds. They hoped that if a guard caught them out of the corner of his eye he would presume they were on a routine mission to assist the cooks or the nurses.

Edek's team inserted the prized key—*it worked!* Quickly they loaded two cases of grenades into the bottom of a wheelbarrow and covered it with some trash. Again, as casually as possible, they strolled back to where the organizers anxiously awaited their arrival. The uprising would begin in a few moments.

Once inside, a few members of the revolt committee inspected the grenades. Though everything appeared in order at first glance, it was soon detected that the grenades—so perilously stolen—had no detonators! They needed to be returned, and before the guards retired to their quarters. Edek and his friends walked back toward the arms room, a little quicker this time. All would be well once they returned the grenades and hid the key again.

As they turned the corner toward the arsenal, something was immediately out of order. A Jewish worker known as a sympathetic informer to the Nazis stood nonchalantly in the hallway. Without missing a beat Edek walked over to the Jew and made up a cockamamie story that Kiewe was looking for him. With Edek leading the informer away from the door and out of sight, the grenades were replaced and the door was relocked.

This event was a terrible blow to the uprising plan, but also an amazing feat that instilled much-needed confidence into the organizers. Their time would come soon.

Chapter 22

Stangl hated to make the announcement but there was no way around it. Before the camp began their cremating operations, the bodies were gassed then buried in large pits at Treblinka. Now they all needed to be exhumed and burned.

"By order of the *reichsführer*, Heinrich Himmler, not only are we to burn the newly gassed bodies, we must now dig up the remains we have buried in the past and burn those bodies as well," Stangl declared to his fellow SS workers.

He looked around and saw the incredible disdain on everyone's faces. It would mean a lot of work. And the smell of burning bodies that had putrefied, or had only half-decomposed, would be ghastly, like inhaling death itself.

It was Otto Horn, a former nurse from the euthanasia program, who spoke up first. "*Kommandant* Stangl, we don't have the equipment necessary. The pits we excavated were fairly deep and—"

Stangl cut him off, saying, "I have thought of that and I have already ordered some heavy machinery to assist us. We have the one older piece, but two more large excavators should be arriving by rail in the next week or two."

"Why this turn of plans?" asked Kuttner.

"Well, for one, the shipments have died down and this will give the workers at Camp 2 something useful to do," replied Stangl. "Essentially this new work will justify keeping them alive. But Herr Himmler's main reason is to prevent anyone from ever finding out what has been happening here."

"Are you talking about—?" Suchomel began.

"Yes. The stories in the press are being used as propaganda to our full advantage to display the evil of communism. Himmler knows that the Soviets will do the same to us should they ever retake Poland."

This statement sobered everyone. Not only was it a shock to realize that, despite all of Hitler's promises, the war had incurably stalled out in Stalingrad and gone against the Germans but also the thought that the Allies would one day overtake Treblinka and discover what the SS guards had been doing. Both ideas were startling and could not be thought of too long.

The distress on the Doll's face said it all.

"Yes, I know it will be a massive undertaking," said Stangl, as if to anticipate Kurt Franz's hesitation. "We are going to have to burn at least ten thousand bodies a day for a month in order to make a dent in it."

"Ten thousand a *day*?" asked Suchomel.

"Yes. The workers at Camp 2 will have to step up. We will augment them with workers from the lower camp. Also, Globocnik is sending over a specialist to help with the process. He should be here tomorrow."

"The reasoning again?" Franz asked as politely as he could, though he was fuming inside. His anger clouded his mind so he could not remember why they were asked to change operations.

"Katyn."

The one-word answer from Stangl was all that was needed to convince the guards.

Earlier that year the German Army had uncovered a ditch, nearly one hundred feet long and fifty feet wide, in the Katyn forest of Russia. In 1940, the Soviets had murdered thousands of Polish officers, stacked the bodies twelve high, and secretly buried them.

Reich minister Joseph Goebbels used the information as propaganda against the Allies. Heinrich Himmler, as Hitler's overseer of the Polish death camps, determined never to let this kind of propaganda happen against Nazi Germany. Thus no mass graves and no evidence to be left behind. The bodies buried in Treblinka during the summer and fall of 1942 would have to be excavated and burned, their ashes disbursed, never to be found again.

★ ★ ★ ★ ★   ★ ★ ★ ★ ★

In Camp 2, Zelo Bloch and Jankiel Wiernik received the news of exhumation soberly. They had no option but to lead the men to do precisely what was ordered. The laborious cremation project began immediately. The lone excavator scraped the soil of one of the mass graves and dug for hours, creating a mountain of dirt between Camp 1 and Camp 2. All of the work finished months earlier to fill the pit and smooth it out was now being undone.

When the cavernous grave was finally penetrated, there arose such a stench of gaseous fumes from the half-decomposed bodies that the workers had to cease operations. Eventually the air cleared a little. After the initial shock, the corpses of men, women, and children were exhumed from the foul ground.

★ ★ ★ ★ ★   ★ ★ ★ ★ ★

A visitor joined the camp to lead the operation. He was an *oberscharfuhrer* with SS insignia on his sleeve. The workers had several different names for him: the *Artist*, the *Specialist*, and frequently he was known as *Tadellos*, which meant "perfect." As he instructed the workers and provided guidance, he had an annoying habit of saying *tadellos* over and over again, even though things were far from perfect in the workers' minds.

The Artist made changes right away. He laughed at the rudimentary ovens they had been using and ordered them dismantled and hauled away immediately. He then had the workers create at regular intervals dozens of cement posts close to two feet high, to be used as pillars. Six sturdy iron rails from the nearby abandoned tracks were laid parallel on top of the cement pillars for a length of 150 feet, forming an enormous grill. The Artist explained that underneath the rails the prisoners should place dry logs and sticks to be used as tinder for the grill.

Once the Artist was satisfied with the measurements and durability of his new roaster, he had the Jewish workers douse the wood profusely with gasoline. Then, as the carcasses were dug up by the excavator, the women's bodies were pulled out, hundreds at a time, and put on as the first layer of the grate. Female bodies, especially the fat ones, were found to burn easier than the males, so they were utilized as kindling.

"*Tadellos, tadellos!*" exclaimed the Artist. In his mind the work so far was flawless.

The excavator pulled out roughly twelve corpses each time it dug.

Zelo, Jankiel, and scores of other men were on hand to yank out the female bodies and carry them over to the grate. After the Artist was satisfied that a good base was laid, he ordered the excavator to put all bodies—men, women, and children from the pit—and lay them directly on top of the women. When there were approximately three thousand bodies, the Jewish workers were instructed to douse it with gasoline over and over again.

Once lit, the entire mound of bodies eventually took flame—a colossal roast of death that the Nazis toasted. As Zelo and Jankiel stood by watching, they witnessed unimaginable scenes of burning horror, which included expectant mothers. With his countenance at a new low, Jankiel thought, *Lucifer himself could not have created a hell worse than this!*

"*Tadellos, tadellos!*" praised the Artist.

The Jewish men had to keep working; never content, the Artist kept suggesting improvements. The Nazis, however, stood by with brandy and cognac. Feeling the warmth from the fire, their bodies and minds were comforted simultaneously, knowing their crimes were being covered up.

The additional excavators arrived and were put to use immediately. Workers were transferred from Camp 1 to help with the project. New grills were made nearby. Soon mounds with ten thousand bodies at a time were engulfed in flames.

The burnings continued. More excavations of bodies, more mounds created. The fire was so hot that it scorched many of the workers trying to manage it. The large flames could be seen from miles away, and anyone within one hundred feet of them would be burned. The noxious odor often incapacitated those who were in the vicinity, including the workers in Camp 1 and the nearby villages. It was awful, even for the guards, who simply stood and watched over the operation. They were permitted to rotate out every two weeks for special leave, to depart from the haunting inferno of Treblinka. But the prisoners were forced to endure.

Eventually hundreds of thousands of bodies had been burned, their ashes scraped into wheelbarrows with a continuous crew of workers depositing their loads in the adjacent fields or the river. Within the ashes were not only bits and pieces of bone, but also jewels and gold that had apparently been swallowed in a desperate attempt before entering the gas chamber. The work was repugnant, hideous, and the workers at Camp 2 sent a message to Camp 1: "*If you do not take action soon, we will take action ourselves.*"

CHAPTER 23

Blonde-haired Tchechia Mandel was told she would not be doing kitchen work that day. One of the maids was sick with typhus, so Tchechia was instructed to perform cleaning duties in the SS living quarters and offices. After breakfast she grabbed her cleaning supplies and departed for that part of the camp, dreaming of the revolt and of one day departing from Treblinka with its memories of Benjamin Rakowski and death everywhere.

When she arrived at the living quarters it was quiet. She cleaned several rooms, removed the trash, and took a quick break before she entered the office area. There was never much time to rest during the day, and the workers were instructed to always run from place to place.

Once inside the *kommandant*'s office, Tchechia wiped down the desk and straightened up the other furniture. All of a sudden the door opened and in walked the *kommandant* himself.

"Why hello," greeted Stangl. "How are you today?"

"I'm fine," answered the startled Tchechia in near-perfect German. She had never encountered Stangl one on one before.

Stangl looked uncomfortable, like he was going to continue the conversation, which Tchechia did not want. She attempted to keep dusting.

"Have you chosen a room for yourself yet?" asked Stangl.

Tchechia stopped dusting. Stangl stood still, looking at her.

"Why do you ask?" answered Tchechia, somewhat condescendingly. She had dealt with these brutes before. She was not too scared to stare at him. Did he want her for himself? Was he trying to flatter her?

"Nothing," Stangl stammered. Her response and tone had taken him by surprise. "I meant nothing by it. I simply wondered if you had been able to move into one of the new rooms we had built for the workers. I can ask this of you, can't I? Why shouldn't I ask?" Stangl became indignant, offended that this Jewish worker would speak to him in the manner that she did.

"May I go?" asked Tchechia.

Again her question startled Stangl, so direct, almost severe. He could tell she was a very smart girl, and one not to attempt to manipulate. He recognized her as the interim camp elder's girlfriend and that she usually worked in the kitchen or at the clinic. *She probably thinks I want to have her for myself now that her boyfriend is gone*, he suspected. "By all means. Go. I am not going to keep you."

Stangl felt ashamed. He knew she thought he was making an advance on her. He also knew that she would have fought him. She was obviously educated, willful, and proud. She had stood up to him like no one else at the camp ever had. He respected her for that, but it also irritated him.

★ ★ ★ ★ ★   ★ ★ ★ ★ ★

"It was terrible," Tchechia said to Bronka. "He just looked at me and asked questions."

"What did you say?" asked Bronka.

"I asked him if I could leave. I wasn't going to stick around to see what he had in mind."

"And you didn't get in trouble?"

"Not yet. I haven't heard anything about it."

Tchechia and Bronka sat in their new room before lights-out. The female workers were taken out of the barracks and given small rooms they shared with one or two other people.

"I could have never done what you did," exclaimed Bronka. "I would have been too scared to even speak to the *kommandant*. They say he doesn't ever speak to workers—essentially doesn't even know they exist. He acts like all this work gets done invisibly."

"Well, he's not as bad as Kuttner or Miete or Franz, but he runs this place, so in my mind he is the worst one of them all."

"He watches things...that is certain. I see him standing on the berm by the tube. He looks down on everyone like he is staring down at his kingdom. He loves to hit the top of his boot with his riding whip."

Tchechia and Bronka sat deep in thought for a moment. The weather was getting very warm. Trains were trickling into Treblinka about once per week. The guards were still selecting passengers out of the masses, but they were sent immediately to Camp 2. The smell originating from the upper camp had been shocking, like death itself. The girls were thankful they had not been *recruited* to work there like some of the other women. Camp 1 was upsetting enough.

Bronka was still working as a seamstress with the male tailors under SS guard Franz Suchomel. There were not as many clothes as before, but each train would bring a large number of bundles to sort through and remove the Star of David. Whenever she could, Bronka spoke to Rudi Masarek about the revolt. There had been informers, traitors who were recently killed in their sleep by the organizing committee, and some who were still working in the camp. There was always news in the camp of *who was speaking to whom*, all in an effort to weed out the informers.

The girls were eager to participate in the revolt. Whatever they were instructed to do they would do it. One request the organizers had for them was that once the revolt started, before they escaped into the woods, they were to use grenades to blow up buildings. This would help the fire spread.

They wanted to leave the camp in the most desperate sense possible. It was hard to think of anything else.

"I keep wondering what we will do when we escape," said Bronka.

"That's not hard—run!" Tchechia replied.

"I know. But we will be in the woods for a while, possibly with wounded people needing care. I know the Nazis will search savagely for us until we are captured."

"Or until the war is over. It is a matter of timing. We have to evade them until the Allies come and take over this part of Poland. Then we will be free. I have heard that the Soviets have started an offensive and are moving west. I intend to find somewhere to hide. We both have money. We should stay together as long as possible."

"I like that idea," said Bronka. "You are much more confident than I am. I can run fast, but I have never traveled without my parents."

"We will be okay," said Tchechia. "We will stay together, and we will be okay."

CHAPTER 24

At Camp 2, the Artist had been at work creating new enormous racks at the edge of the large pits housing the remains of bodies killed in 1942, before the cremations started. Each pit contained tens of thousands of corpses at a minimum, and the largest one held nearly one hundred thousand. Even after a pit was cleared of bodies there would sometimes appear to be some blood in it. When this happened, a Jewish worker would strip naked and descend down into the pit to dig around and look for any additional body parts that were not captured by the excavator.

Next to one of the larger pits where ninety thousand to one hundred thousand people were buried, the Artist created a specially designed rack where up to thirty thousand bodies could be placed at once—ten times the normal amount. All was going well with his plans until a ferocious gust of wind caused the flames to spill over and leap into the mass grave, which ignited immediately. As onlookers stood by, they noticed how the burning blood pooled near the surface, like petrol, intensifying the heat and flames so that over sixty thousand bodies in the large pit were burning at once. The Nazis cheered.

★ ★ ★ ★ ★   ★ ★ ★ ★ ★

A train made its way into Treblinka station on a warm, sunny morning. The pitiful souls who emptied out of it were the remnants from the Warsaw ghetto. They wore just rags for clothing and had little to no valuables. A few of the women from Warsaw were pulled out from the passengers and sent to Camp 2 to help in the kitchen. They were so distraught from what had happened in the ghetto that it took three days to calm them down enough so they could speak intelligibly about what they witnessed. They described it as complete annihilation.

Of the other passengers, the men and women without any children were sent straight into the tube. For some reason, unknown to the workers, the mothers *with* children were marched up to Camp 2 by the Doll. When Kurt Franz arrived with his Warsaw prisoners of women and children, he marched them to the rim of the large pit, which was burning out of control.

The Nazis stood there and seemed to enjoy the terror-stricken faces of the toddlers and their mothers, as if it was a sport. Then the Doll and other SS men began grabbing the children and throwing them into the fiery pit, to the torture of their mothers, who passionately begged and pleaded with their captors. These mothers were being given *special* treatment because they had been some of the last out of Warsaw…and perhaps part of the resistance.

As the women stood there wailing, the Nazi men tormented them, saying, "Why don't you jump in to save them? Are you cowards?"

Most of the women were now on their knees, clutching tightly to the remaining children and pleading with the guards to spare them, but to no avail. The ones who were not thrown alive into the flaming pit were marched up to the edge and shot so they would fall in. Of the onlookers whose turn would be next, many fainted and were dragged to the edge by a guard and then thrown in. The screams from the pit were bloodcurdling.

While this was occurring in the upper camp, the husbands and fathers were beaten with rifle butts as they transitioned from the tube and entered the gassing rooms. They were packed in at record numbers and allowed to suffer in the stifling hot chamber for a while. As they yelled and shouted, the Nazi guard in charge of the diesel engine decided to wait and have another drink of whiskey first. This way, the victims could experience the full wrath of what was to come.

★ ★ ★ ★ ★   ★ ★ ★ ★ ★

Thankfully for the workers at the upper camp, a message arrived for Zelo from Camp 1. *"The revolt would begin in days."*

PART 4

THE REVOLT

CHAPTER 25

In the throes of a hot summer, the work of Treblinka at Camp 1 practically ceased. The Warsaw ghetto had been cleaned out, some arriving on trains wounded with bayonet stabs, and some already dead. Though Camp 2 continued to remove bodies out of the ground for cremation night and day, Camp 1 was in desperate need of activity.

Kommandant Franz Stangl decided to perform one more big construction push to keep the laborers occupied. Old roads were resurfaced. New roads were paved. Signs were created for every corner of the camp. New fencing was put up. Decorative carving took place on some of the larger buildings where the Nazis lived. The Sunday shows were still conducted, but there was stifling, dry heat to deal with, not to mention an ever-present malodor that was revolting.

Stangl was determined to keep everyone working hard to impress Odilo Globocnik and Christian Wirth, his regional supervisors. The new construction projects would keep the workers busy and validate Treblinka's existence, but it was a challenge for everyone. None of the SS wanted to be there and some of the Ukrainian guards deserted. The stench was too much to bear.

Stangl knew that without people entering the camp to be processed, Globocnik could shut down their entire operation on a whim and order the camp to be leveled. This would inevitably mean the death of all of the Jewish workers, a command he would be reluctant to issue.

That was when a large group of Gypsies arrived…on foot, with horses pulling wagons full of goods. The workers watched as hundreds of Gypsies poured through Treblinka's gates. However, it did not take long to process them. The passengers had no idea what their future held. Within a few hours all of them were gone, their bodies incinerated.

★ ★ ★ ★ ★   ★ ★ ★ ★ ★

The revolt date came but nothing happened. A train had arrived with many additional Ukrainian guards as escorts the exact morning the revolt was scheduled to take place. The organizers decided to put it off a few more days.

That summer, Richard Glazar and Karel Unger were tasked onto the camouflage unit to go into the woods and bring back juniper branches for the fences. It was a highly organized mission, where the men were divided into groups, each with a foreman and SS guards for security. On one occasion, they returned to Treblinka but were ordered to enter the back gate of Camp 2. None of the Camp 1 inmates had ever seen the pits, or the gas chambers. It was quite a sight for Richard and Karel to digest.

Out of the corner of Richard's eye he recognized Zelo in a group of Camp 2 inmates who were laboring adjacent to the closest pit. Though he looked changed, it was definitely Zelo. His skin was blackened from working near the fires all summer, and his face appeared gaunt, but he still had that command presence Richard admired. His shoes and pants were soaked with blood, and it looked like he was shepherding men as they scraped ashes out from under the large grills.

Zelo glanced toward Richard and recognized him as well. A friendly exchange took place among the two Czechs while they silently searched each other's eyes. Richard noticed something urgent in Zelo's expression. The end had come, everyone knew it. In a few days the Camp 2 workers would complete the exhumation mission and finish disseminating the ashes. As a result, the SS guards would surely kill them all because they were witnesses to the crime. Some action had to be taken immediately, like the very next day—that was the tidings Richard received from his nonverbal exchange with Zelo.

But then, as if needing confirmation, Adasch—standing beside Zelo—shouted out in Yiddish for all to hear: "What are you waiting for? Everything is finished, isn't it?"

Richard, Karel, and their entire foraging crew from Camp 1 understood exactly what that meant. They returned to their barracks and explained to Rudi what happened.

"We will revolt this week!" Rudi exclaimed. Then he called together

Edek and some other young men to make sure they understood how important their task to break into the arsenal would be.

Rudi defined for everyone the three main goals for the revolt: First, to set fire to all the buildings, which would destroy the camp; second, to kill all the SS and as many Ukrainian guards as possible; and third, to escape into the woods and, if possible, to free the Polish men and Jewish prisoners held in a penal colony nearby the main camp, sometimes referred to as Camp 3. There was no contact with the workers at Camp 3, so the forced laborers would have no early warning of the revolt. However, Zelo and Galewski thought it would be advantageous to kill the guards at Camp 3 as well, so they could not act as reinforcements to search the woods after the revolt. Rudi agreed. There were so many conditions that needed to take place in the first few moments of the revolt for it to be effective, it was hard for Rudi to keep them all in mind. Night after night he had gone over all the details with his fellow conspirators.

★ ★ ★ ★ ★   ★ ★ ★ ★ ★

In Camp 2, the Nazis began to celebrate. They had whipped and beaten the inmates to such a degree that the speed of the work was greatly increased. Over six hundred thousand bodies had been exhumed, and they were now excavating the final pit using two excavators. They would be done soon, so they decided to have a toast toward their accomplishment. They planned a banquet for that evening, sort of an early celebration supper. Zelo and Adasch found it ironic that the Nazis would celebrate, yet it was the Jews who had done all the work.

One of the excavators was broken down and needed repairs, but it appeared they were no longer concerned with fixing it. They had almost completed the mission. One of the main duties now was discarding the ashes. The process was to not only sprinkle the ashes out in the field, making sure there were no bony fragments in it, but also to replace some of the ash back into the deep pits to be covered over with a layer of sand. Soon the soil would be graded down, the ashes completely disbursed, and the mission would be over. All they would have to do was burn the new bodies arriving for processing, which would only take a few hours once they were removed from the gas chambers.

Zelo sent word through the carpenter Jankiel that the revolt must take place within the next twenty-four hours.

★ ★ ★ ★ ★   ★ ★ ★ ★ ★

Rudi Masarek was now pressed for time. It was Sunday, August 1st. There were still several items that needed to be done, yet he would honor Zelo's appeal. It was decided the revolt would take place the following day at 5:00 p.m. The plan was to use the arms room depot key to steal the two cases of grenades with their triggers, along with a few rifles and ammunitions, in the early afternoon. After those items were secured, there would be no turning back from commencing the revolt.

The first group of men in action would surround the barracks and cut the telephone wires. Then the Ukrainian guards were to somehow be lured away from their posts, possibly with a twenty-dollar gold coin, before grabbing their weapons and shooting them. Grenades were to be thrown into the German command post and other places where the Ukrainians and SS might be milling at the time of the revolt. Besides blowing up the gassing chambers, all the wooden buildings were to be doused with gasoline and set on fire, and the armored truck was to be taken over and used to shoot at guards.

In addition to the disrupting events, one contingent of inmates was to focus on the sadistic SS guards like the Doll and Miete and liquidate them as fast as possible. Another contingent would eradicate the Ukrainians on the guard towers. And several men were to focus on opening the gates that faced the forest for a mass escape.

A single shot, fired at 5:00 p.m., was the signal to begin the revolt. One serious problem to consider was the difficulty of having that many anxious men and women make it through the day without giving away any clues. Too many people were in on the plans, and they had not yet dealt with all the informers. There were approximately six hundred Jewish workers left in the lower camp and two hundred in the upper camp. The revolt had to be synchronized. If they were discovered early it would mean many of them would die in the *Lazarette*.

Forty of the men had previous military training. Rudi was counting on this fact for some assurance their scheme *could* work. Still everyone was edgy. The workers knew that the next day they would either escape or be killed. There was no other option if they participated in the revolt. Camp elder Galewski made his rounds, reassuring everyone and encouraging them to remain calm and prepare mentally for the next day.

★ ★ ★ ★ ★   ★ ★ ★ ★ ★

In the women's quarter there was never much talk of the revolt, chiefly due to the effectiveness of a couple of female informers. Therefore the women were not officially told when it would start, but they could tell it was imminent due to the way the men were acting. Tchechia received the clues with a measured response. She knew which workers could be trusted and which ones could not. There was a female *kapo* who lorded it over the women each day. She was a known informer. Her name was Paulinka.

Paulinka and Kuttner Kiewe had an understanding. To that date in August, Paulinka had given away at least six Jews who had mistakenly confided to her they had plans to escape. She was despicable, and Tchechia speculated that Paulinka was probably the reason the men felt they could not trust her and Bronka with too many of the details. *Someone should take care of her first*, thought Tchechia.

Bronka caught a quick glance from Rudi during the Sunday afternoon camp performances. It was the type of look that communicated that he had some important information for her. He did not smile, or even hold the gaze for very long, but without a shadow of a doubt, Bronka knew what it meant. The revolt was inevitable now.

Bronka thought for a moment. It was comfortable standing there, listening to the concert. The guards had treated them better in the last few weeks than they had earlier in the year, when trains flooded Treblinka's unloading platform with passengers. It almost seemed wiser not to revolt with how well the guards were treating them, but Bronka knew the *comfort* she now felt was fleeting. Besides, what would happen when the war ended?

Bronka knew that all of the workers would have to be killed because they could not be left alive as witnesses to the murders occurring there. Bronka reassured herself that the revolt was the only way forward, the only plan that could move her out of the cycle of slave labor followed by death. She and Tchechia would participate in the revolt and escape—or die trying.

Tchechia was stronger than her, both emotionally and physically. Bronka realized she might die while trying to flee the guards, while Tchechia would more likely make it safely to her freedom. These thoughts were a little terrifying for her, but she knew she could not be paralyzed by fear. That fear in itself could cause her death if it prevented her from taking a risk on the most important day.

When the concert finished, the young women ran next to each other back toward their living quarters, where they would wait until supper. Before they arrived, Bronka whispered to Tchechia, "The revolt is happening tonight or tomorrow."

"How do you know?" asked Tchechia.

"I could see it in Rudi's eyes."

"Well then, we must get ready. We will make sure the gold we have stored is easily accessible once we hear the first shots being fired."

"I hope we have enough," said Bronka.

"It will have to be enough!" declared Tchechia.

★ ★ ★ ★ ★   ★ ★ ★ ★ ★

Zelo could not sleep. At dark, the male barracks in Camp 2 was locked and the lights were turned off soon after. The men knew what was happening the next day through communication between some of the workers across the fence. It was clever how they did it, but it *had* to be clever or the Germans would find out what was going on. The revolt was to begin at five in the afternoon, and Zelo and his men would be ready.

★ ★ ★ ★ ★   ★ ★ ★ ★ ★

Before Franz Stangl settled down for the night he thought about writing a short note to his wife. It was his usual routine, a habit he had started many months before. He did not always mail the letters he wrote to her, but he usually wrote and updated her on how he was doing and asked her questions.

However, that night he was deciding against writing her. He had just returned from leave. His wife Theresa had pestered him incessantly about quitting his post. She had somehow figured out what was happening at Treblinka, and that "her Paul" was in charge. It had greatly disturbed Theresa. She recently saw a priest about it. Her final words to her husband before he left home was that he needed to quit, and soon. *She did not understand*, thought Stangl. *It was not that easy.*

Stangl put down his pen. He would write her tomorrow night.

A sip of liquor.

A moment to think.

In essence, Theresa had issued him an ultimatum, though she knew she wasn't allowed to do that to him. He had gone over this with her after they were first married. He could issue an ultimatum, as the man, but she was never to give him one. She did not like that rule then, and she obviously did not like it now, because she threatened him. It was almost as if he were supposed to choose Theresa over his job at Treblinka. It wasn't fair.

She knew he couldn't simply quit, not with men like Globocnik and Wirth. They had no feelings for others, and it appeared no sense of family, or what it might be like to be married to a strong-willed wife. These were men who had a singular focus—deal with the Jews.

Stangl decided to take his mind off the whole mess. He would definitely not write Theresa tonight, and he would consider writing the next day. *Tomorrow will be a good day*, Stangl thought. A friend from Vienna passing through the area was to visit with him over lunch. *It will be nice to catch up*, he thought. *But for now I must get some sleep.*

CHAPTER 26

Monday, August 2nd, was a very hot day. The guards discussed several tactics on how to keep cool, but finally decided they would take a nice long swim after lunch. Stangl received his visitor and began drinking with him before their meal. The Doll had taken a pass to leave the blistering hot and smelly work site. He would not be back for a few days.

Several of the Jewish workers walked along the camp street, watering the parched flowers. The rest of the Jews were at their respective work sites, keeping out of the sun and trying to act normal. There were no trains that morning. Just stillness, except in the upper camp where they feverishly worked to finish operations.

Before lunch, while smoke rose from the grills in Camp 2 and Ukrainian guards walked the perimeter fence for their morning rounds, Rudi told the young men to take the cart to the munitions room.

"Now is the time," he said softly. "May God be with you."

The young men had been briefed that they *must* secure the grenade detonators this time, and they were ready for the task. Just before they left, however, it was reported that one of the guards whose room was directly next to the arms room had worked the previous night and was now resting inches away from where the young men were to gather the rifles and grenades. Something had to be done. Camp elder Galewski, who spent the morning reassuring the workmen who were having a hard time focusing, dispatched a brave worker to go and deal with the untimely predicament.

The man selected by Galewski went to the guard's room and knocked furiously. "Sir, you must arise! You are needed in the vegetable garden. There is a fight with the potato workers."

The guard arose, swore, dressed, and then rambled out of his room to attend to the problem.

"We must move quickly," the worker declared to the guard. It was true; time was of the essence.

When the Jewish worker and the guard departed the area, a horse and cart—the one used for garbage pickup—was rolled up to the back of the ammo room. One of the men went through the front door with the stolen key and then opened the back window next to the cart with trash. The grenade boxes were handed out the window, as well as the detonators, pistols, and then rifles.

Nearly three dozen weapons passed hands through the window and were then quickly wrapped in burlap and placed underneath the garbage moments before a desperate whisper was heard. "He's coming back! Quick, get out of there!"

The young man inside the room lowered the window, replaced the bar, and hurried out of the room. As he rounded the corner of the building, he passed beside the grumpy guard who was frustrated by being called from his rest for such an insignificant matter.

The horse-pulled cart made its way over to the SS garage managed by Standa Lichtblau. The mechanic inspected the grenades and weapons. They were ready for use. He took the munitions and a secret stockpile of alcohol bottles out of the garage. Working stealthily, he disbursed everything by wheelbarrow to other work sites. By the time lunch was over there were weapons and grenades all across Camp 1.

Galewski told Rudi, "The nest is out. Get word to Zelo. From this moment, not another Jew will be murdered without reprisal!"

★ ★ ★ ★ ★   ★ ★ ★ ★ ★

Tchechia sat in the kitchen area, peeling a mountain of potatoes with three other women, when there was a quiet knock on the door.

"Is Paulinka here?" a male voice asked when the door was cracked.

"No, she is at another site."

Standa quickly entered the room, bringing half a dozen grenades and detonators. He looked at the women seriously but with a slight glow emanating from his eyes.

"It is today," he said triumphantly. "Hide one of these grenades in your potato buckets."

"Gladly," said one of the workers. Tchechia reached out a second time to have two grenades for her bucket.

★ ★ ★ ★ ★   ★ ★ ★ ★ ★

Zelo and Jankiel received the news from Camp 1 with relief. Their crew was scheduled to be locked in the barracks that afternoon, but Zelo convinced the guards to let them all continue working for extra bread rations. The cremation work needed to be done, so the guards relented.

Zelo inspected the weapons and ammo previously bought from nearby peasants. The revolt was to start at 5 p.m. He eyed the guards on the watchtowers along with those in the excavators. He would be ready.

The Jewish workers at Camp 2 had desperately waited for this day. Having endured incredible mental suffering with their scandalizing tasks, they were filled with much relief to hear the good news. The workers had only to withstand but a few more moments. They labored heartily, trying to act normal, yet whispered to each other in passing, "*Ha-yom, ha-yom!* (The day, the day!)"

★ ★ ★ ★ ★   ★ ★ ★ ★ ★

Stangl and his Viennese friend were laughing, having a grand time. They had finished lunch, but the stories and drinking continued. They could be heard from outside Stangl's office.

Some of the guards congregated under the branches of a large tree on the edge of the courtyard. Another group of guards departed for their afternoon swim. Suchomel, in a bright-white shirt, decided to ride his bicycle around the camp for a while. Miete and Mentz rested in the shade at the *Lazarette*. Kiewe, his hat pulled low over his forehead, was dispensing ten lashes as punishment to someone who displeased him. He did not know that his actions were being watched very closely by attentive prisoners.

★ ★ ★ ★ ★   ★ ★ ★ ★ ★

Richard observed the wonderful, cloudless blue sky as Rudi gathered the Czech contingent around him. He was so nervous and overcome with emotion that he could barely speak.

"Has the gasoline been sprayed on the buildings by the disinfectant detail?" Rudi asked. The worker in charge of spraying all the clothes with disinfectant had a central part to play for the entire plan. He filled his canisters with the gasoline received from the garage and walked around the camp that day, spraying the sides of all the buildings.

"Yes, check."

"Everyone on the list has their guns or grenades handy?"

"Check."

Rudi wiped the sweat from his brow. "The gas pump will blow up as soon as the first shot is fired?"

"Yes, as well as the buildings around it."

"The branch cutters are ready to cut the telephone lines? People are at the fence, ready to blow it open? Galewski is keeping an eye on Kiewe?"

"Check, check, check!"

Rudi gave the men a genuine smile, the first one seen from him in a long while. As he spoke his final words he was borderline incoherent. "Boys…tell the ones at home…this is the moment…"

Rudi shook each man's hand one last time: Robert, Richard, Karel… but Hans refused to shake. He quickly mumbled something about the revolt not actually happening.

Hans had seen revolt dates come and go; he did not want to get his hopes up too high that day. Something had changed about Hans after Zelo had been taken to Camp 2. It seemed he could never quite pull himself together, and he was not as helpful to the revolt organizers as he had been when Zelo was with them. The other Czechs recognized that something had broken inside of their friend; they understood his despair.

David Brat grabbed Richard's hand and whispered to him, "King David's psalm declares, 'Yea, though I walk through the valley of the shadow of death, I will fear no evil, for thou art with me.'"

Richard held firmly to David's hand—a true friend. Richard remembered when he was delirious with typhus and suffering from malnutrition. David came to the sick bay and secreted two small, wrinkled apples into Richard's hand. How much David spent for the apples, he never cared to share. What Richard could not forget was after David gave him the apples, the old man knelt down and kissed Richard on the forehead. It was a simple gesture, but in a place like Treblinka, where the only physical touch was with a whip or a slap, the kind act was truly remarkable.

Other workers shook hands, always discreetly, and always in the knowledge that it could possibly be the last time they would see each other. There was a glow in everyone's eyes and a spring in their steps. Bellies were stuffed with food for the long night; pockets were stuffed with money.

As the minutes ticked on, spirits grew agitated: 2:10, 2:22, 2:37... Galewski and Rudi determined they would not be able to wait until 5 p.m. to begin the revolt—something would most definitely happen before then. Though they wanted the time to be as close to evening as possible to aid the workers' escape under the cover of darkness, it was decided that 4:00 p.m. would be the new time. Galewski sprang into action to let Camp 2 know about the change.

The heat was intense.

Suchomel took another lap riding his bike.

Laughter was heard from the *kommandant*'s quarters.

Then something happened that put everyone on edge.

Shouting was heard from behind the barracks...

What was up?

Kiewe discovered a teenager with a pocket full of gold. He began inspecting other men near him, telling them to clear out their pockets. Kiewe shouted for Blau, one of the chief *kapos* who was friends with Stangl and an informer. The two began discussing what had been happening that day—boys shaking hands at lunch as if they were saying goodbye, workers being especially nice, men running to formation quicker than usual...

Suddenly Kiewe began marching one of the men caught with gold toward the *Lazarette*.

It was not yet 4:00 p.m., but something had to be done. Galewski sent a man with a pistol to intercept Kiewe.

A shot rang out.

The camp froze.

CHAPTER 27

At Camp 2, the men heard the shot but it was earlier than expected. They were not sure if it was the revolt or one of the many executions at the *Lazarette*. The men, soaked with perspiration and blood from their duties, paused for a moment, glanced at each other, and continued to work. Then there were explosions and more shots. The uprising had started! It was time to take action.

Zelo hurried to a wall where a sharp axe was hidden, camouflaged in the corner. He then ran toward the nearest guard, who stood looking at him in disbelief. One strong swing to the midsection and the guard went down. Another guard came running. Another swing. Zelo had his second kill. He grabbed their rifles and handed one of them to a fellow worker.

Others at Camp 2 went into action. Adasch and Jankiel ran to retrieve their pistols and let the men in the male barracks know the revolt had begun. The workers outside who had been carrying corpses quickly grabbed whatever they could find: pitchforks, shovels, and other instruments used for their dreadful tasks. They immediately put them to work on the bewildered guards.

Soon men were being killed on both sides, guards and workers. Both guards driving the excavators were shot. Guards in the towers were targeted, but they returned fire, and some with deadly accuracy. The months of pent-up anger and rage from the Jewish workers at Camp 2 finally released itself upon the guards who had whipped and threatened them daily.

Several men started cutting through the multiple layers of barbed-wire fences that separated camp work and freedom. There were three rows of barbed wire plus an additional row with trestles interspersed with barbed wire.

One row cut through.

Two rows cut through.

One of the guard towers not out of commission yet began firing down on those cutting the fences.

More shooting.

More cutting.

Bodies were prostrate all around the fourth and final obstacle before freedom. Soon the tower gun was quieted. An immensely loud explosion originated from Camp 1. The Ukrainian guard in the tower decided to escape down the stairs and run for his life.

The gas station has blown up!

Zelo knew it was time to flee and join the main effort at the lower camp. The workers here would finish it up. *No more bodies would be excavated today!*

★ ★ ★ ★ ★   ★ ★ ★ ★ ★

Kiewe heard the crack of a gunshot, then felt a searing pain in his left side. Had he been fired upon? By whom? Who dared? He fell to the ground on his side and looked up into the face of the man who had shot him. There stood a Polish worker named Wolowanczyk, a Jew from Warsaw. *He actually had a confident grin on his face!* Kiewe wanted to scream to warn Mentz, but it was too late.

When he heard the shot, Mentz came quickly out of the *Lazarette*—he, too, was shot. *Something has to be done and quick*, they thought. But neither were able to get up and do anything. It appeared the inmates had taken over the camp.

★ ★ ★ ★ ★   ★ ★ ★ ★ ★

Kommandant Stangl jackknifed out of his chair and shouted, "What the devil is going on out there?"

As soon as Stangl opened wide the door to his office, gunfire sprinkled the exterior wall of his building—almost as if it was directed at him!

"Who is doing this?" Stangl shouted.

Stangl's visitor leapt for the floor and hid behind the desk. Stangl, as if in a daze, clumsily shut the door and locked it, then maneuvered to the floor alongside his friend. Whatever was happening outside, they would have to wait it out.

★ ★ ★ ★ ★   ★ ★ ★ ★ ★

"Kiewe's got his!" a voice yelled out.

"Hurrah!" shouted another voice.

"Revolution!"

Immediately after the single shot on Kiewe there was a brief pause, as if no one could comprehend what was happening. Though it was a quarter hour before 4:00 p.m.—fifteen minutes before the prescribed time—Galewski quickly deduced that the workers must immediately follow through and continue what had been started, even if the upper camp was not ready. Without words passing between the two men, Rudi understood the same and went into action.

To get things going, Rudi whipped a grenade out of his pocket and thrust it in the direction of the Ukrainians' barracks. *Kaboom!*

He then secured a confiscated machine gun and climbed to the top of the zoo's pigeon house for a good vantage point. It had been a while since he had been a lieutenant in the Czech Army, but his warrior instincts were now fully engaged.

Jews with pistols and rifles from each camp now came running into the courtyard, looking for guards to fire upon. Franz Suchomel quickly un-holstered his pistol and began firing into a mass of workers heading his way. The workers with guns immediately returned fire, knocking Suchomel off his bike, but they did not fatally wound him. He clambered away toward the mess hall.

Bottles of petrol turned into Molotov cocktails were lit and thrown at many of the wooden buildings, instantly setting them ablaze.

Grenades exploded.

Machine-gun fire rattled throughout the camp.

More shots, more explosions, more yelling.

"Hurrah! Hurrah! It's begun!"

Several gasoline drums were set on fire, causing enormous explosions and black billowing smoke. It did not take long for the SS and the Ukrainians to realize what they were up against.

Those in the watchtowers began to rain down violent gunfire onto the Jewish workers. But their gun blasts drew attention from the armed insurgents and the guards soon became targets themselves. Grenades were lobbed at the towers, machine-gun fire was returned to their high positions, and some of the tower guards were taken out.

As the Jewish workers ran out of ammunition they threw their weapons to the ground and looked for fallen guards to steal theirs. Chaos ensued as the uprising was now in full swing.

★ ★ ★ ★ ★   ★ ★ ★ ★ ★

The potato workers in the kitchen did not hesitate to jump into action with their weapons. They knew exactly what they were expected to do. Seizing the grenades from their buckets, they ran outside and witnessed the full extent of the revolt.

As Galewski had earlier instructed them, the women dispatched their grenades toward the guard buildings and offices. Nearly everything ignited in instant flames. The dry, dusty weather finally aided the workers who had endured the scorching heat each day.

Tchechia was exuberant. She ran up to one of the wounded Ukrainian guards and grabbed his rifle. As she moved out she directed her rifle forward and led the women in shouts of, "Die you Nazi pigs! Hurrah!"

A few of the female workers, excited with their initial success, were now expected to head to Stangl's office to set it ablaze, but they were stopped by gunfire and explosions. One woman was shot and fell where she stood. The other women, now terrified of dying, wanted to immediately flee the camp before it was too late.

Tchechia, wishing she could cause more damage, turned the corner away from a blazing building and sought to head toward her friend Bronka, who had been on the other side of the camp when the revolt started. More blockades and withering gunfire hindered Tchechia's way.

She and a group of women ran across the courtyard, away from the explosions. As they scurried about, a few of them came face-to-face with Paulinka, the informer.

"Hey, Paulinka," shouted Tchechia. "Did you betray people before you came to Treblinka, or just take up the skill here after you arrived?"

Paulinka stared back at the group defiantly.

Another woman, who had lost her sister to Paulinka's disloyalty, rushed past Tchechia with a large rock in her hand. In precious little time the woman paid Paulinka back for being a traitorous informer. She had no regrets.

The roof of a building crashed down next to the cluster of workers. They searched for an avenue of escape but instead saw Nazi reinforcements entering the camp. They could not go in that direction, and they could not escape through the burning buildings.

Then suddenly, out of a dark cloud of smoke, Franz Suchomel appeared. He approached the women and declared, "If you come with me now back to the kitchen, I will ensure your safety and see that no reprisals come your way."

Tchechia looked at the tall fence still blocking her way of escape. There were Nazis standing in front of it, shooting at people running toward them. Tchechia thought of Bronka, who quite possibly had already left the camp. She thought of what might happen to her if she hesitated in answering Suchomel.

"Okay," Tchechia responded. She and several of her brigade followed the lone SS officer into the mess hall and laid down on the floor to ride out the storm.

★ ★ ★ ★ ★   ★ ★ ★ ★ ★

Bronka looked for Tchechia but couldn't find her anywhere. Then she tried to find Rudi but saw that he was on a roof, shooting at the guard towers. She recognized fallen comrades all around her, and heard others screaming, "Flee, flee, before it is too late!"

Bronka ran with a group of men into Camp 2, where she had never been allowed entry before. They snuck alongside the grilling racks and an enormous pit, partially filled with bodies. They made their way over to a watchtower that was being consumed by flames. She and several men climbed over a fence and through an anti-tank barrier that had been manipulated enough by others for a passageway. *One more fence to get through!*

Bronka noticed several dead bodies lying around an opening in the fence, men who had given their lives for others to escape. She quickly ran through it, then proceeded into the woods beyond.

★ ★ ★ ★ ★   ★ ★ ★ ★ ★

Richard held unbridled joy as he ran to and fro, carrying an axe, shouting, "Hurrah!" He couldn't believe the Ukrainian barracks were burning to the ground. Warehouses, garages, and shops throughout camp were all burning. Guards were being shot, but unfortunately far more Jews were going down.

Richard ran alongside his friend Karel, who was waving a spade over his head. Suddenly Karel stopped. Just twenty yards in front of them was a guard, poised behind a tree, using a rifle to take out workers running past him, one by one.

Robert Altschul, coming up from behind, ran past Karel and Richard without realizing the danger ahead. *Crack!* The Czech with a razor-sharp analytical mind fell facedown in the hard dirt like a rag doll, shot dead by the guard.

Keeping their emotions in check, Richard and Karel turned to flee in the other direction. As they maneuvered away from the armed sniper they heard a familiar voice, shouting, as if to push them on. It was Rudi. Still on the roof. He was yelling at the Nazis while he fired his rounds in their direction.

"Take that for my wife!"

"Take that one for my unborn child who did not even get to come into this world!"

"Take that, you murderers!"

Richard noticed the fake train station that Stangl commissioned and on which Jankiel Wiernik spent countless hours working. It was now engulfed in flames. He scanned the area, looking for Hans, but he was nowhere to be found.

As Richard and Karel kept running, Richard laid eyes on Zelo. He had apparently opened the gate between Camp 2 and Camp 1 and was helping workers cross into the upper camp to escape for the woods. His commanding presence was easy to spot as he was giving orders like a true leader. Zelo maneuvered swiftly to help as needed—engaging the enemy with his rifle—all the while simultaneously encouraging those around him to be brave and fight back.

Richard knew he may never see Zelo or Rudi again, but he also knew he must keep moving with Karel. Nazi reinforcements kept showing up out of nowhere. Something told the young man he better not hesitate or he would be shot from behind by the crisscrossing barrage of fire.

Utter confusion.

Explosions and smoke.

Lack of order.

All the meticulous planning to ensure that hundreds of Jews could escape had evaporated into a burning mess and a barrage of bullets reigning down on them from the towers and other fortified positions of the guards. Regardless of the plans, it was now time to make their escape because the Nazis were overwhelming the camp with gunfire.

"Outta here! Outta here! Get into the woods!"

Poor Robert!

Where was Hans?

Would Rudi get down from the roof and escape?

Zelo!

CHAPTER 28

Franz Stangl looked out his window at the chaos in his camp. His beautiful eight hundred meters of flower-lined street was littered with bodies and smoldering debris from the fires. The new guardhouse, built exquisitely with wood in Tyrolean style, now burning down! The new fuel pump and tank, designed like a real service station with flowers and signage, had gone up in a massive explosion, which blew out some of the surrounding buildings' windows.

His new barracks—gone!

His new street—in ruins!

The bakery whose Viennese baker made such delicious treats—blown up!

His beloved train station with the imitation clock—burning like an inferno!

One of the guards from Camp 2 had escaped Zelo's wrath and banged on Stangl's window.

"The upper camp is overrun!" he shrieked. "Everything is burning—the men's barracks, women's barracks, and the kitchen."

Stangl wasted no time getting on the phone to call the chief of the external security police. "Revolt! Come quickly!" He was thankful the telephone wires had not been cut. Then he loaded his pistol and ran outside to see if he could find any Jews causing more destruction to his beautiful camp. *Did they not consider all the planning and the time it took for construction?*

★ ★ ★ ★ ★   ★ ★ ★ ★ ★

The Jewish workers still fighting knew they were on a suicide mission. They continued to clear lanes of passage for their fellow workers to escape through. There would be no hope for those still firing at the Germans

128

once reinforcements arrived. In addition, special units were sent on patrol in various distances to scout the perimeter of the camp. The longer those still sacrificially shooting waited, the less odds they would have to escape.

Known informers were dealt with, much like Paulinka, who had her head shattered. Eventually some men broke through the bars of the carpenter's workshop window and ran around to open up the fence with their axes. People stormed through the gate, but it was quickly blocked again. Upon hearing the initial explosions, immeasurable Nazi reinforcements poured through the railroad gate of Treblinka. One of the first places they tried to defend was the gaping hole in the gate.

Bodies—mostly of Jewish workers—littered the open spaces of the camp. Nearly every building seemed to be on fire. The heat from the flames hungrily torched everything around it, including humans who ventured too close. The only hope now was for those who had already crossed over Treblinka's gates.

Rudi Masarek lay mortally wounded on the roof of the pigeon house. As soon as he ran out of ammunition he became an easy target for a sniper in one of the guard towers. Unbeknownst to his friends, Rudi had decided long before that he was not going to leave Treblinka. The revolt needed people who would continue to fire to provide clear lanes of passage so the utmost people could escape. During his dying breaths he thought of Gisela and the life they intended to have together.

Hans Freund, like Robert, was shot during his escape toward Camp 2 and the woods beyond.

With caked blood on his shoes and pant legs from his work amidst the pits, a persistent Zelo led with zeal and moral stamina. A rampant fearlessness and concern for others compelled him to leave the safety of Camp 2 and its gateway toward freedom, so he could help his comrades at the lower camp.

He was last seen running in and out of the flames, exhorting fellow workers to take courage, return fire, and flee for safety. Sometime along the way, Zelo Bloch was riddled with bullets and cut down by the might of a machine gun. He poured out everything he had until he fell.

Camp elder Galewski made it to the upper camp alive. He assisted other workers at great risk to himself to ensure they made it over the barbed wire encircling Camp 2. He struggled to pull every worker he could through the danger area and into the safety of the woods.

★ ★ ★ ★ ★   ★ ★ ★ ★ ★

In the lower camp, Suchomel, Tchechia, and the other women who had sheltered in the kitchen were suddenly forced to flee the building when the roof caught on fire. A swell of frightened workers congregated in the camp yard near to where the female sleeping barracks were burning. Surrounded by flames and a storm of gunfire, a panic set in on all who had fled there.

A guard's voice penetrated the clamor and confusion. "Put your weapons down. There will be no reprisals for those who form up in front of the *kommandant*'s office. I repeat, put your weapons down and make a formation in front of the *kommandant*'s office. Those who comply will be spared. Those who resist will be shot. There will be no reprisals for those who peaceably move to the formation."

At this point, the frenzied mass of bodies halted and complied.

The revolt was over.

If one was not already through Treblinka's gates, there was no option but to cease the uprising—resisting was useless. Besides the guards inside the camp, the Nazis had surrounded the perimeter at a distance of five kilometers.

One hundred and five prisoners formed up in front of Stangl's office. They had survived the revolt, but they were still prisoners of Treblinka.

Tchechia was unable to make it to safety. She held out hope that Stangl and Suchomel would keep their promises. She decided to search for a new way to escape, possibly alone, as soon as the commotion died down.

All evening long, those who remained at Treblinka heard gunshots, dogs barking, and shouting from the woods. More and more Jews were rounded up and killed. *Hopefully Bronka made it into the forest and survived,* Tchechia thought.

★ ★ ★ ★ ★   ★ ★ ★ ★ ★

Camp elder Galewski fled through Camp 2 as one of the final workers to get through. He—like Zelo—continued with all his might to push and motivate workers not to give up, to keep moving, to keep fighting, to never lose hope. He found himself in the woods with a few other escapees in the late afternoon, going from person to person, urging everyone to keep moving because in the morning the Nazis would round them up if they didn't move. He worked himself to exhaustion. Alas, when it was time for he himself to get up and continue the journey, utterly depleted, and with Nazi guards quickly closing in on his position, camp elder Galewski ingested a vial of poison from his pocket. Within seconds he was dead.

★ ★ ★ ★ ★   ★ ★ ★ ★ ★

Go, go, go! Bronka kept quietly repeating to herself. She tried hard to keep up with those men who were just in front of her. She was exhilarated. Unbelievably, against all odds, Bronka had made it outside the perimeter fence and beyond.

Once inside a densely packed area of foliage, the small contingent of escaped workers halted so they could hear if any trucks were coming. The only sounds were the machine-gun noises from the camp piercing through the forest. They decided to continue to head southwest; there was an ancient logging road nearby. Bronka noticed there were seven workers in her group, and there was another larger group of approximately twenty ahead in the distance. The larger group went to the right and followed the old road. Bronka's group decided to stay in the trees and follow a creek. Dogs would surely be sent to hunt them down, so they kept in the water wherever it was available.

Moments later there was shouting a few hundred yards away, horses were heard, and vehicles with mounted machine guns, all trying to chase down the escapees. Bronka's group waited, not wanting to cause any movement. It was not dark yet, and the trees were not as thick as they wanted.

The seven survivors watched as the Germans and Ukrainians infiltrated an area where they suspected a mass of Jews were hiding…and they were correct. Men came out with their hands up, but they were mowed to the ground by crisscrossing fire. Bronka's group slowly crawled away from that area as quietly as possible, seeking denser brush and a place to wait for nightfall.

More yelling.

More vehicles heard in the distance.

More gunshots.

Would the sun ever set? Bronka wondered.

They saw the nearby peasants all run for their homes, not wanting to be mistaken by the Nazis as Treblinka workers. Bronka's small contingent spotted an old barn on the edge of the woods. Some wanted to creep inside to wait for the sun to set.

Four men ran for the barn, but Bronka stayed with the two other men. They ran another kilometer and a half deeper into the woods, away from the barn, and decided to climb into three trees, thick with branches and foliage to hide them. Bronka rested in her branch and wondered what might have happened to Tchechia.

Unfortunately Tchechia had been in the wrong part of the camp when the revolt started. Bronka easily escaped into Camp 2, but Tchechia would have had to scale over a high fence or break through the back wall of the buildings that separated the female living quarters with the sorting areas of the camp. Bronka searched in vain for her friend as other small clusters of people barreled through the woods. But there was not even a sign of other women, let alone of Tchechia.

The three workers hiding in the trees heard a terrible sound in the direction of the barn. German voices. Screaming. Machine-gun fire. Bronka was thankful she had decided to keep moving. She held tightly to her tree, hoping the guards would not come in her direction.

CHAPTER 29

Richard Glazar and Karel Unger ran next to each other, shouting, laughing, and jumping for joy. They had crossed the vegetable garden, ran by the smoldering racks in Camp 2, and then exited Treblinka through the fallen gate.

Gunshots penetrated the air around them, bodies fell, people cried, but Richard and Karel kept running. After the fence came the woods, those glorious woods that meant *freedom*! Yet they knew the woods would be viciously hunted that night for any sign of survivors.

The two men slanted left, then ran across a weedy field toward the bogs. Another man was just in front of them. All three ran through the dense bushes surrounding the shore and jumped into the water.

Swimming furiously, the man in front of the Czechs reached the other shore first. *Crack!* A gunshot from a dark-uniformed guard on the opposite side mowed down the poor soul who had tasted a short-lived liberation from Treblinka. The gunman wasted no time and pointed his rifle toward the two men stalled in the middle of the lake. *Crack! Crack!*

Richard and Karel dove low down into the water, scraping the silty bottom, swimming furiously underwater back toward the shore they had just left. Richard raised his head among some reeds he thought might be used for cover. *Crack!* The guard spotted his ascent. It was target practice. Richard plunged back underwater. In the brief second he grabbed a mouthful of air, he saw more weeds, thicker cover, out of the corner of his eye. He swam there, hoping Karel would make it as well.

Inside the willow branches Richard risked another breath. More shots, but not nearly as close. *It must be at Karel!* Richard plunged back under the water and slipped to the thickest area of reeds. A hand grabbed his arm. Richard barely raised his face out of the water—it was Karel, grinning at him. They had made it!

There were a few more shots, as if for good measure, but the sun had lowered under a distant tree line. A grey hue hung over the bog. Treblinka was in a mountain of smoke. The men stayed in the water until it was almost completely dark, twilight, with only their faces out to draw another breath. They were alive and wanted nothing more than to flee the area, but they heard shots everywhere around them.

All of a sudden there were voices heading their direction. Dogs barking, people shouting loudly, drawing near to their position. Several horses galloped by the bog.

More shots!

More shouting!

More horses!

It was as if the Nazis were right on top of them.

"Over here," one of the guards shouted. "There are two more bodies over here!"

A truck rumbled in behind the submerged escapees. Their adversaries were within ten feet of where Richard and Karel had buried themselves in the reeds and willows, having only the top of their face above water.

"Park it here!" one yelled. The Czechs could hear the Nazis hoisting dead bodies into the flat bed of the truck.

The dogs kept moving, away from the area.

"Let's hurry, it's almost dark," one of the guards bellowed.

The truck departed.

More shots were heard, away from the bog.

Richard and Karel had not been detected. It was just murky enough in their patch of the bog to escape notice.

As a dragonfly danced around the still faces of the two Jewish friends, the concluding glimmer of daylight evaporated and darkness flooded the area. The Czechs wait for another hour—their faces ravaged by mosquitos—delaying their departure because of the truck returning to the camp. More voices. More dogs barking. The wagon, full of dead prisoners who had dared to hope for escape, slowly rumbled back to Treblinka. All through their time in the water, the two men could hear machine-gun fire, pistol shots, and rifles—the furious sounds of reprisal and death waiting for them if they, too, were found.

Agreeing it was time to move out of the water, Richard and Karel swam to the distant shore and crawled out of the slippery mud on the bottom of the bog. Submerged in the water for over four hours, they were soaked and shivering. Before they ventured into the woods they looked back at Treblinka to see it still ablaze with multicolor flames. Good riddance.

★ ★ ★ ★ ★   ★ ★ ★ ★ ★

As the two men navigated through the trees away from camp, they could still hear gunshots in various places around them. They were cautious to avoid areas of light, and stayed away from where there was any activity. Karel was barefooted. His shoes had been lost in the thick mud of the lake's bottom. The two men searched for them before they departed, but the shoes were lost forever.

Long before dawn they considered stopping, but decided against it. The more distance between them and Treblinka, the better. They followed the stars and moved in a generally southwestern direction for hours, avoiding farmhouses and roads. When the sky began to lighten with the breaking of the dawn, the men hiked alongside a farmer's mowed field. They found some dense bushes and gathered a mound of freshly cut hay to bed under. Utterly depleted both emotionally and physically, their exhausted bodies soon found undisturbed sleep.

Near sundown the men awoke and considered their position. They had traveled away from the flames of Treblinka all night, but now what? They did not have a strategy beyond their escape. Should they depart Poland and head into Slovakia? Should they look for a town and claim to be Gentile workers of the resistance? The answer came to them when they stumbled upon a peasant woman who declared that all prisoners of war should head west, not east. The two men were traveling in the wrong direction!

They agreed their star navigation was deplorable. They had been walking toward the Russian advance! No wonder there had not been any Germans on their tracks; they had been going the wrong direction, but perhaps it was fate.

Karel suggested to Richard, "The Lord is with us. He has his hand open to us."

Karel's sentiment proved right when the two slipped into a barn one night to bed down in the straw up in the loft. There was something hard beneath them—*apples!* "Again," suggested Karel, "the Lord has provided." They ate from the secret apple stash until they could stomach no more. Richard began to accept Karel's conclusions.

In the morning, they decided to make up false identities. After staying a while in their providential barn refuge, they fled west toward Warsaw and the Vistula River.

CHAPTER 30

Back in Treblinka, though the uprising was extinguished, the chaos lingered. *Kommandant* Stangl's phone rang continuously; guards called in the numbers of Jewish workers who had been rounded up and shot, and higher-ranking officers from headquarters asked about the status of supplies, and if Treblinka needed more backup. Stangl handled all the important calls. One thing he was blessed with was an even temper; he would survive this, even if other people were spinning out of control all around him.

"No, we do not need any more reinforcements," repeated Stangl to a Nazi on the other end of the line. "What we need now are basic supplies. We will have to rebuild. All the dormitories for Jewish workers are burned down."

The man on the other end muttered something.

"No, they are not all dead. We have over one hundred here who need a new barracks," Stangl explained.

The calls about the reprisals were the most common. Stangl had an assistant scribble down numbers on a notepad placed near the phone. Soon the record showed that more Jews had been shot than had escaped. *That couldn't be! Something is wrong. They are starting to kill the villagers by mistake!*

Realizing the situation beyond the perimeter of the camp had gotten out of control, Stangl issued the order that all the reprisals should stop immediately. "Return to camp!" he ordered.

Soon he received the phone call he had been dreading. It was from Globocnik.

"Report to me immediately!" Globocnik grumbled and then hung up without waiting for a response.

Stangl had no choice but to oblige.

★ ★ ★ ★ ★   ★ ★ ★ ★ ★

When Stangl entered Globocnik's office at the SS HQ in Lublin, he was sure he would be fired on the spot. But it was not the case.

"Operations will be shut down immediately," snarled Globocnik. "Your work there is terminated."

Stangl stared at his supervisor and nodded silently.

"Further, I want all the remaining structures bulldozed, the land plowed over, and every trace of Treblinka abolished from the earth. Do you understand?"

"Yes, but why——?"

"This is not going to be another Katyn Forest story. Himmler is very clear on that point."

"But I thought I would rebuild," Stangl suggested. "I have bricks and other materials——."

"Not at all. There will be no rebuilding. Effective immediately you are no longer the *kommandant* of Treblinka. Kurt Franz is the new *kommandant*, and his only role is to tear it down, plow over it, and plant flowers and pine saplings. This will be a farm when the Soviets find it."

"The Soviets?"

"Yes! The Soviets. You know by now how things are going in the east. We have to move out. Relocate. In fact, I have your next assignment for you. You are to return to Treblinka only to pack your bags so you can report to Trieste."

"To Italy?" asked Stangl.

"Yes, you will report there for your new duties in an anti-partisan combat unit on the Italian front. I will be going there as well. And so will Christian Wirth. It is time for you to move on from here. We are shutting down most of these camps."

"What of the workers who remain at Treblinka?"

"They are to stay there for now," answered Globocnik. "Then, when they have served their purpose to assist with Treblinka's transformation, they will be shipped to Sobibor, or shot."

His words rattled Stangl. He had given the remaining Jewish workers assurances that they would not be put to death. He had hoped to rebuild Treblinka, better than it had ever been. But he could now see that the *larger war* was calling the shots. Globocnik and Himmler were looking at strategy, public relations, and propaganda on an international scale. Stangl had been focused on the operations at Treblinka. He, and the Jews who worked for him, were collateral considerations and not important to the grand strategy.

When Stangl traveled to Lublin to meet with Globocnik he was fearful he would be reprimanded for the revolt. Now he could see how foolish his thinking had been. Globocnik was Himmler's chief lieutenant for the extermination centers in Poland that were about to be overrun by the Soviet Army. Day-to-day happenings in one concentration camp such as Treblinka were nothing compared to the very real possibility of Germany losing the war. What was at stake was their entire way of life. If Russian tanks and soldiers conquered German forces in Poland, there would be nothing left to stop the Allies from conquering Berlin and all of Germany.

From that moment on, Stangl knew that he had to think about his future, about Theresa and the children. If he hoped to ever have a life with them, he must begin preparations immediately. Europe was drastically changing.

The countenance of Globocnik when he spoke of moving from Poland was unmistakable depression and defeatism. There was no more fight left in him. The war would be lost, and what had happened at camps like Treblinka needed to be hidden. "Did you account for all of those who escaped?" asked Globocnik.

Stangl knew what he meant by the question. Globocnik wanted to be assured there were no survivors, no witnesses to the mass killings that took place each day at Treblinka. He was tempted to lie and say that he believed all of those who escaped had been shot, but something about the entire mood in the room that afternoon suggested the era of playing games was over. Now honesty was more important than posturing.

"I have no idea," Stangl replied. "How could I ever know? There were hundreds who fled into the forest, and hundreds who were reported shot. Were they the same people? There is no way to know."

Globocnik stared at him listlessly. The curt response was not what he expected from Stangl. He made no reply, just sat at his desk and stared straight ahead.

Stangl began to feel uncomfortable. Should he leave?

Suddenly Globocnik turned toward him and said, "You have no more than three days to clear your post." Then he motioned with his hand that the visit was over.

Stangl departed and closed the door behind him.

★ ★ ★ ★ ★   ★ ★ ★ ★ ★

At Treblinka, the first order of business was to collect the bodies strewn across the camp in order to burn them. The Jews had to work extremely hard to make up for all of those workers who had escaped or perished in the uprising. Since most of the Jewish workers at Camp 2 had been killed in the initial fight, nearly all of the remaining males were tasked to assist in the upper camp with the final excavations of corpses and the burnings.

Unfortunately those who planned the revolt neglected to ensure the demolition of the building that was target number one and absolutely essential for them to permanently destroy—the gas chamber. It was made of brick and withstood all attempts by the workers to set it ablaze. Within a few hours the facility had been repaired and was ready for operation.

Tchechia was desperate for information. With no worker leadership, the Jews were forced to rely on whatever the Nazis told them. She looked for another opportunity to escape, but it seemed there were more SS and Ukrainians in the camp than there had ever been. She remained hopeful that Bronka had escaped alive. She knew that on the day of the revolt her friend was on the side of the camp nearest to Camp 2, where workers found an avenue of escape. Tchechia searched for her intensely, but thankfully she did not find her among the deceased who were unloaded from the camp trucks that returned from the woods.

Three days after the revolt, Stangl assembled all the workers in the courtyard. He was departing and he wished to say goodbye to all of them. He gave a short speech, then actually stepped down off of the porch where he normally stood and approached the workers. He began to shake the hands of those who were familiar to him.

"Good luck," Stangl said with a restrained smile. "I'm sure you will be leaving here soon yourself."

Kurt Franz, the Doll, stood to the side, glaring at the spectacle. This was not proper Nazi protocol, and it would not make things easier for him with the job he had to do. The camp was closing down. That meant the remaining prisoners would have to be liquidated.

Stangl departed the area.

Franz now stood before the assembly and told them to get to work.

Less than two weeks later, seventy-eight freight cars from Bialystok containing 7,600 Jews unloaded on Treblinka's large platform. Though there was no warehouse to sort clothing, the tube and gas chambers were still able to serve their purpose. The passengers were commanded to immediately strip and run down the tube for a shower. Soon the large diesel engine was activated, rumbling until the deadly mission was complete.

★ ★ ★ ★ ★   ★ ★ ★ ★ ★

Stangl and Suchomel traveled side by side in a long military convoy along with Odilo Globocnik and Christian Wirth in separate trucks. They were accompanied by a few of the Ukrainian guards from Treblinka to provide security for them. Some of the trucks were transporting storage containers bursting with diamonds, cash, and other valuables. The men who had carried out Himmler's secret plans in Poland were now dispatched to the front lines in Italy. They were sent together, for better or for worse, to provide leadership to a large concentration camp near Trieste.

★ ★ ★ ★ ★   ★ ★ ★ ★ ★

After the revolt, Tchechia became the leader of the few women who were left. They cooked, they cleaned, and they laundered the clothing of their Nazi taskmasters. They did not know what to expect from day to day. Multiple rumors circulated the camp about what was to be their fate.

There was another Jewish worker at the camp also named Tchechia, a young woman who became known as Little Tchechia. Little Tchechia would speak to Tchechia after lights-out, fearful that they could soon be forced to enter the tube and be gassed after all the buildings had been torn down. Tchechia told her not to think of such things.

When October arrived and the temperature was not nearly so blazing hot, the camp had been transformed. All of the burned buildings had been excavated and cleared. Even the brick buildings were bulldozed over, with lorries of wagons removing the debris from the premises. The fake train station area had been dynamited. It was obvious the time for departure had come.

On October 20, 1943, an empty train pulled into Treblinka station. Most of the Jews were loaded for resettlement. No one who had seen the events at Treblinka would be allowed their freedom. They realized that meant being incarcerated at another concentration camp where they would probably die.

One of the guards told Tchechia and Little Tchechia not to board the train, along with one other woman and two dozen males. There were still a few jobs that needed to be done at Treblinka before the SS departed, and they wanted the assistance of a remnant of workers.

"Why didn't we board the train, Tchechia?" asked Little Tchechia.

"I don't know," Tchechia responded.

"Where do you think the others are going?"

"I heard they are going to Sobibor," Tchechia responded plainly.

"Sobibor? Isn't that another place like this one?"

"Yes, I've heard this."

"What are they going to do with us?"

"Don't fret. Perhaps we will find out tomorrow."

"How can you be so strong? This may be the last night we live and you act like it is nothing."

"It's not nothing; I just choose not to worry about what I cannot change."

"I wish I was more like you," Little Tchechia whispered, nearly asleep.

The third female worker listened attentively to their conversation.

★ ★ ★ ★ ★   ★ ★ ★ ★ ★

Another day passed.

After finishing their daily work for the Nazis, the Jews were locked in two empty railcars at night. The buildings had been demolished, and all that was left was a small homestead where the SS lodged. The hours passed slowly.

Each day felt so uncertain, which was horrifying for the men and the three young Jewish women. Suddenly ten of the male workers were taken to a makeshift *Lazarette* in the woods. Five were shot in the back of the neck with a Finnish submachine gun set to semiautomatic. The other five men awaiting execution were ordered to place the dead bodies onto the grill before it was their turn—the workers' final act of service to the regime.

Another uncertain night.

Another painful morning. At daybreak the Nazis discovered that one of the male prisoners had hanged himself in the railcar. The remaining male Jewish workers were disposed of at the same location in the woods as their comrades, dubbed the "new" *Lazarette* by the Nazis.

A night.

A morning.

A train sounded in the distance just before noon.

There was a small room in the homestead where the SS ate their mid-day meal. Kurt Franz walked in and saw his men being served by the three female workers.

He eyed Tchechia and smiled.

Tchechia instantly knew what was about to happen, but she observed Little Tchechia very diligently pour water into the cups of her captors. Tchechia watched as the Nazis sat and curiously stared at their server. Little Tchechia did not know what was coming.

Suddenly the Doll cleared his throat and said, "Well, girls, it's your turn."

Little Tchechia dropped the pitcher.

Tchechia busted out with mocking laughter and declared, "Aha! I never did believe your fairy-tale promises of freeing us. You pigs! Just do me a favor and don't ask us to undress!"

Little Tchechia whimpered, then began to cry.

With gritted teeth Tchechia turned to Little Tchechia and said, "Don't cry, Tchechia! Don't do them the favor. Remember, you are a Jewess!"

It did not help.

Little Tchechia wept all the way to the woods.

The Doll instructed the three girls to kneel facing a pit where the remains of the male bodies were still smoldering.

Tchechia whispered to herself, "These lying pigs—"

A gunshot rang out, shattering the silence.

Little Tchechia screamed.

Another shot echoed in the forest.

Whimpers disappeared like mist in the wind.

Crack! One final shot.

Silence.

Franz picked up a few dry sticks and threw them on top of the three bodies to stoke the fire. He dusted off his hands, then walked away.

The last Jew was killed at Treblinka.

POSTSCRIPT

Dusseldorf, West Germany
1964 (Twenty-one years later)

Fifty-year-old Kurt Franz—agitated at being named in the indict-ment—was one of ten men who had been charged with war crimes at Treblinka.

I shouldn't be at fault for anything! Franz thought. *I was just following orders, and never hurt anyone. I didn't even belong to the Nazi party!*

Sitting through weeks and weeks of testimonies, everybody from a train dispatcher to a handful of Jewish witnesses who escaped, Kurt Franz was at a boiling point and wanted to share his side of the story. His attorney would not let him.

On one of the days, Samuel Rajzman testified about the Doll's involvement in escorting prisoners to the *Lazarette*, and also lying to people entering the tube by telling them they were going to receive a shower. He further explained how Franz would have his attack dog Bari tear to pieces innocent Jews who just happened to come across their path.

"Lies!" Kurt Franz could not contain himself any further. He yelled aloud in the courtroom, "Pure lies! I've never killed another person!"

People at the trial howled their disapproval at the outburst. *Did Franz really think anyone would believe the suggestion that he was innocent?*

The judge told Franz to shut his mouth, and that there was to be no more outbursts. Rajzman continued, explaining that the Doll suspended Jews from their feet to whip and torture them before he pulled out his pistol to end their lives. More sadistic stories with incredible detail and poise were told. Rajzman was a very convincing witness.

The next person to testify was Richard Glazar, now a forty-four-year-old engineer from Prague. He methodically explained to the courtroom the deceit and lies propagated by the Doll—from the fake sick bay painted with a sign of the Red Cross to the assurances given to those supposedly walking toward the showers. Glazar grimly diagrammed the camp to the court and showed where everything was located, including the gas chambers, the mass graves, and the burning pits. He elaborated on the trains that would empty out and how the masses were herded into the tube toward their death.

Glazar spoke of his own fate, that only a handful of men from the masses arriving from the Theresienstadt Ghetto were allowed to survive. The rest were sent to their deaths often within minutes of arriving at the camp. He systematically discussed how Kurt Franz tortured and killed prisoners on a daily basis. His detailed analysis as an eyewitness was irrefutable, yet Franz continued to protest, saying he was barely ever at Treblinka and he did not partake in any of the violence.

Glazar specifically explained how, in November of 1942, Kurt Franz, in his gray deerskin gloves and skull and crossbones cap, shot seven prisoners with his pistol for trying to escape, and when he ran out of bullets he borrowed Miete's pistol to finish the job. He also explained how Franz killed a worker with a shovel.

Another defendant, survivor Abraham Kolski from New York, testified how Kurt Franz and an unnamed guard each grabbed babies left outside the gas chambers by their mothers and smashed their heads against a wall. To this charge, Franz knew he must respond. He composed a letter and had it delivered to the judge. It read, *"On this day, allow me to send this sworn statement that I have not killed a single person. Never on my orders was a Jewish worker harmed."*

Bronka Sukno, deposed in Israel, was also a witness for the prosecution about the camp and the guards. She recounted how Franz beat the camp doctor, Julian Chorazycki, to death, and then kept beating him even though the man was clearly dead.

While the transcript of her testimony was delivered, the Doll remained unfazed and maintained his innocence. "I was a true soldier," Franz bemoaned. "I never intentionally hurt anyone."

"Stop!" the judge demanded. "That is an insult to every person who *was* a decent soldier! Your behavior has nothing to do with being a soldier. No more outbursts!"

Karel Unger did not travel to West Germany, but a delegation of the court was sent to interview him at his home in Seattle, Washington. Like Glazar, Unger spoke on the conditions in the camp and of the atrocities of the Nazis, now sitting as defendants. He described Kurt Franz as a macabre man capable of the worst devilry imaginable.

"Kurt Franz was like an animal," Unger shared. "When he saw blood he became wilder and wilder. I would describe him as a sadist."

Unger went on to share about the death of Chorazycki, and spoke specifics about seven other people who Kurt Franz specifically killed in Unger's presence. He shared in the same way as Glazar, matter-of-factly and precise, with testimony that corroborated what others had described.

When the transcript of Unger's testimony was read in Dusseldorf, Kurt Franz threw a fit and made a public display. "Never in all my life have I harmed anyone!" he protested. "I do not know why these lies keep being told about me."

At this, the judge nearly lost his composure. "Don't act this way! Or is it your position that all the witnesses have it out for you, and that you are the most harmless and kindest of them all?"

No response from Franz.

During the trial, the defendants had been able to keep the semblance of a united front. They were not killers, they were acting as soldiers and following orders; that it really bothered them when they had to discipline one of the prisoners.

However, as the trial progressed, the coalition of Miete, Mentz, Suchomel, and Horn began to unravel. The lawyers for Miete and Mentz decided to argue that the defendants might have killed a few hundred workers, but it was only under duress. Suchomel flat out admitted he argued with Franz and Kuttner about them killing a specific male worker he wanted to keep alive, an obvious effort to show that he (Suchomel) was trying to side with the prisoners.

The lawyer for Kurt Franz did not admit to any killing. He held that Germany and its political society were to blame for what took place at Treblinka, and that Franz was simply a loyal instrument carrying out his orders but not hurting anyone intentionally. This failed tactic was attempted at the Nuremberg trials…with similar results.

On September 3, 1965, the verdicts were read at the Dusseldorf court. One of the ten men was acquitted, Mr. Otto Horn. Horn claimed he worked at Treblinka under duress from Odilo Globocnik and Christian Wirth, and that his frequent requests for reassignment were denied. He kept himself drunk to block out the evil. He would volunteer for the night shift and then sneak off to find a comfortable place to sleep and shirk his duties. Since there were no charges of brutality and murder attributed to him—in stark contrast to the other defendants—Horn was acquitted and did not serve time.

One Nazi named Heinrich Mathes, the guard in charge of the Camp 2 death and burial operations, was charged with the murder of at least one hundred thousand people and sentenced to life imprisonment. Franz Suchomel, along with four other Nazis, was charged with aiding and abetting murder. For this, Suchomel received a seven-year prison sentence.

Kurt Franz, August Miete, and Willi Mentz were charged with "murder in concert" of at least three hundred thousand people. Mentz, as Nazi overseer of the *Lazarette*, was additionally charged with aiding and abetting murder of twenty-five people and sentenced to life imprisonment. Miete, known in the camp as the Angel of Death, was additionally charged with the murder of nine people and sentenced to life imprisonment.

Unfortunately for Kurt Franz, his pleas of innocence did not endear him to the court. Besides "murder in concert," he was additionally charged with the murder of 129 people and sentenced to life imprisonment. It especially outraged those in attendance when he claimed he intentionally assisted the revolt organizers by leaving a loaded machine gun for them on his bed when he departed for leave that August day.

A prevalent narrative had developed in the jurors' minds throughout the trial and came to fruition when evidence was presented as a result of a pretrial police search. Authorities entered the Doll's apartment following his arrest and searched his premises. The investigators found a photo album the Doll had created, which contained many scenes from Treblinka, such as the fake station, the zoo, the *kommandant*'s quarters, and several of the workers. Franz had labeled the album *"Die Schonsten Jahre Meines Lebens"* ("THE BEST YEARS OF MY LIFE").

★ ★ ★ ★ ★   ★ ★ ★ ★ ★

Adolf Hitler's rise to power resulted in 18 million battle deaths, and an additional 20 million civilian deaths. When I think of these numbers, I am forced to pause and consider just how many human lives they represent, and how many families were torn apart. Nearly every country in Europe was devastated by Hitler's ideological fanaticism. Poland itself lost 20 percent of its entire population during the war, and the German Reich killed outright over three million Russian POWs.

Hitler seethed in nationalistic ideals that held deep racism, bigotry, and hatred for others. Unfortunately this attitude was mimicked by many of his chief lieutenants, including Heinrich Himmler, Reinhard Heydrich, Odilo Globocnik, and Franz Stangl: the first two men with their extermination planning; the last two who physically built and oversaw Operation Reinhard death camps.

Operation Reinhard was a code name given for several extermination facilities in Poland. Never before had German concentration camps been used to liquidate entire populations en masse. The operation was named by Himmler as a tribute to his deputy Reinhard Heydrich. Himmler's chief lieutenant was murdered just as the three camps he envisioned at the notorious Wannsee Conference were becoming operational. This top-secret meeting at Wannsee, Germany, was organized by Heydrich and included plans for the industrial-scale use of poisonous gas (instead of shooting squads) to eradicate millions of European Jews. No more would the Nazis talk about shipping Jews to Madagascar. This top-secret Nazi plan was known as the Final Solution.

After Heydrich's death, Himmler followed up as chief organizer and decided to use veteran SS police men such as Odilo Globocnik, Christian Wirth, and Franz Stangl—confidantes who had proven themselves as effective administrators in the German euthanasia program called T4. Stangl was first ordered to go to Sobibor by Globocnik in the spring of 1942, but this lasted less than half a year because Treblinka was in such desperate need of good leadership. Globocnik trusted Stangl, and the Austrian did not let him down. Soon after arriving to the camp, Treblinka became fully operational and able to *process* between five to ten thousand people during normal operations, with a peak capacity of eighteen to twenty thousand per day.

No one is certain how many people perished at Treblinka because no records were kept on those who died there. The numbers range from 900,000–1.2 million people. The sole eyewitness to all of the trains that passed through Treblinka was a railway dispatcher, Franciszek Zabecki, who worked for the Polish resistance. Zabecki swears to the fact that there were 1.2 million people whose lives ended at Treblinka. To better understand this number, it represents the current population of Dallas, TX, or the entire state of Rhode Island—wiped off the map in one year, at one small camp (Treblinka was approximately fifty to sixty acres in size).

Compared to the estimated 1.1 million lives lost at Auschwitz, Treblinka might have disposed of more bodies, and in a more compacted timeline. The loss of one innocent human life is tragic; the losses accumulated at Treblinka are too monstrous to comprehend. *How can one account for such evil?*

The inspiring part of the Treblinka story is the revolt.

On August 2, 1943,
without help from anyone outside the gate,
with no inside knowledge of current Nazi planning,
with just a few guns and hand grenades,
a group of men and women,
in a desperate attempt to seize onto life,
organized an insurrection against their Nazi overlords.

How their hearts must have burned that day! Of the approximately eight hundred workers left at Treblinka on August 2nd, it is estimated that half were killed during the revolt, one hundred surrendered, and of the two hundred to three hundred who broke out of the camp, most did not survive the first night. Of the 100–125 workers who were able to flee the area (August 1943), only a mere sixty-seven workers survived the entire war (May 1945).

Before the Russians retook Poland, the Nazis effectively made Treblinka disappear. Besides a few bone fragments left in the surrounding soil, there remained absolutely no trace that this insignificant-looking rail stop contained the location of the most efficient execution center during the Holocaust. Only because of the revolt, and the survivors who were fortunately able to testify at the war crimes trial (albeit twenty years later), were nine Nazis—the worst and most heinous at Treblinka—convicted of war crimes. Only one was acquitted.

In contrast, at the three-day Belzec trial there were eight defendants, but only one was convicted, and he for a mere four and a half years. Imagine, a sentence of less than five years at a location where five hundred thousand Jews were murdered. The reason is very plain: only one survivor from Belzec remained to give an eyewitness account to the atrocities there. At the Treblinka trial, there were dozens of surviving witnesses thanks to the revolt and the near seventy heroes who survived the war, such as Richard Glazar, Bronka Sukno, and Karel Unger.

Richard Glazar's story is truly remarkable. As chronicled in his book *Trap with a Green Fence*, after he and Karel crossed the Vistula River the two men were arrested and held as prisoners for weeks in a cramped cellar. They finally convinced their captors they were workers in Albert Speer's "Organization Todt" and were trying to return to Germany. Karel used the name Vladimir Frysak, and Richard used the name of his Treblinka friend, Rudolf Masarek. The two Czech men ended up back in their homeland but were forced to work as laborers, then transported to Manheim, Germany, to work in a factory.

After the war, Glazar studied in Prague and became an engineer in his homeland. During the Cold War, Glazar was looked upon with suspicion under Stalin's iron curtain, and he was declared an undesirable. The Communists forced him to perform manual labor at a steel plant from 1951 to 1953. After this experience, Richard and his family escaped to Switzerland, where he lived for many years. Karel became a chemical engineer in the Pacific Northwest of the U.S.

Bronka Sukno spent the rest of her life in Israel. A delegation of the court consisting of judges, prosecutors, and defense counsel met with her in Tel Aviv in February 1965 to record her testimony. Thus the story of

Suchomel shooting a mother to obtain a doll her child clutched was part of Bronka's deposition.

Zelo Bloch, Tchechia Mandel, and Rudi Masarek (who went to Treblinka deliberately out of his love for Gisela) were all remembered fondly by both Jewish survivors and some of the Nazis who guarded them, such as Franz Suchomel. There was something in their spirit that embodied leadership, independence, and hope. Both Franz Stangl and Franz Suchomel remembered Tchechia with much respect. In interviews, Richard Glazar continually credited Rudi and Zelo with the success of the revolt. In a similar vein, the six Czech friends were looked upon by the rest of the camp with near adoration.

One of the Polish Jews, David Brat, told Richard Glazar, "You must survive; it is more important than that we should." This elite status made the Czech men very uncomfortable, thinking it made them a target for Nazi retaliation, but there was nothing they could do to diminish that certain aura and esteem they held within the camp. Unfortunately the fate of David Brat remains a mystery; it is assumed he died in the revolt, along with Edek.

For the Nazis, at the conclusion of the trial in Dusseldorf, Franz Stangl's whereabouts was still unknown. The Treblinka *kommandant* was apprehended in 1945 and investigated for his work in the euthanasia program at Hartheim. He disguised his duty assignment at Treblinka from the American investigators. After two and a half years, on May 30, 1948, Stangl broke out of prison in Linz, Austria, and escaped into Italy by foot.

Stangl eventually emigrated to Syria for three years, then to Brazil. He lived happily with his wife and daughters until he was found by Nazi hunter Simon Wiesenthal and extradited in 1967—twenty-two years after the conclusion of WWII. Stangl was charged with the mass murder of nine hundred thousand people. Due to some technicalities he was only on trial for his time at the Treblinka death camp, not Sobibor. The trial took place in West Germany from May 13 to December 22, 1970. Stangl was sentenced to life imprisonment. He died in prison on June 28, 1971, during his appeal, but only after concluding a remarkable series of interviews with journalist Gitta Sereny. After weeks of meeting together, Stangl finally confronted his guilt and verbalized it with Sereny: "But I was there...so, yes…in reality I share the guilt…because my guilt…my guilt…" Stangl died of heart failure just hours after uttering those words.

Incredibly Kurt Franz, similar to Stangl, lived for fourteen years unmolested in his native city after the conclusion of WWII before being apprehended. He began his life sentence at the trial's conclusion in 1965, but he was released early from prison for health reasons in 1993. He lived for another five years, never acknowledging his many crimes. As the lead prosecutor at Dusseldorf, Alfred Spiess put it, "With Kurt Franz there was no remorse or inner realization."

Kurt "Kiewe" Kuttner somehow survived his shooting during the revolt. He recovered from his wounds and went on to live for another two decades, without any retribution. He died in 1964, mere weeks before the commencement of the trial in Dusseldorf.

★ ★ ★ ★ ★   ★ ★ ★ ★ ★

One aspect especially important to consider with Holocaust studies is the behavioral aberrations among both the Nazis and the Jews. For the Nazis, there were a few men who were particularly kind to the Jews in a *betrayal* from the dictates of Himmler, Globocnik, and Wirth. As described in this book, Franz Suchomel had his moments of kindness with the workers he supervised. Sadly, in a final summation, an evil apathy kept him at Treblinka, making him complicit in all the SS war crimes.

A more startling example of Nazi kindness was found within an SS man named Karl Ludwig, who spent time as a guard at both Treblinka and Sobibor. Two survivors, Joe Siedlecki from Treblinka and Ada Lichtman from Sobibor, recounted that Karl Ludwig was terribly kind, regularly bringing the workers gifts of food, which no doubt saved many Jewish lives.

On the other side, there was this type of betrayal in the Jewish community as well. Some of the Jewish men and women betrayed their fellow workers to the Nazis. These people gave away countless innocent lives to an evil regime ever hungry to learn of a potential uprising, whether true or not. These two aspects are rarely covered, yet eerily present within the camps.

One very noteworthy element of the Operation Reinhard trials was the emotional struggle of the survivors. First, they had to willingly cooperate with the officials by providing their historical accounts to investigators. And second, most of them physically showed up and were present to testify against their tormentors, who were also physically present, staring back at them from the dock inside the courtroom.

In one instance, a man named Moses Rapaport, who arrived at Treblinka in a sealed railcar, testified about his pregnant wife and eleven-year-old son. After exiting the railcar, Moses escorted his slow-moving, very-pregnant wife to her line. All of a sudden two shots rang out, dropping Rapaport's wife and his son onto the unloading platform. Apparently they were not moving fast enough.

While Rapaport shared his personal account to the hushed assembly, Kurt Franz stared at him with a broad grin. At one point, Rapaport looked up into the crowded courtroom and laid eyes on Franz. He leapt to his feet and then fell backward, down into his chair, unconscious. He was rushed out of the courtroom in a wheelchair and taken to a hospital, the victim of a circulatory collapse.

Before Rapaport had finished his testimony, another survivor named Abraham Bomba bolted from the courtroom, sobbing with hands over his eyes. He, too, had arrived at Treblinka with his wife and four-week-old baby. His family encountered a similar fate. Those who testified must have certainly been traumatized, having to relive their experiences in front of their tormentors, now sitting as defendants. I am in awe of their bravery.

The emotional trauma inflicted by their Treblinka experiences affected the survivors long after the war ended. Two of the men who outlived the revolt tragically took their own lives years after the war. One Jewish worker who revolted was Hershl Sperling. After the uprising, Sperling survived multiple other concentration camps, including Auschwitz, and was eventually liberated by U.S. soldiers at Dachau in 1945. However, while living in Scotland in 1989, he jumped off a Glasgow railroad bridge and into the Clyde River.

The other suicide victim was Richard Glazar. Unable to cope with the loss of his wife, Glazar jumped out of a high apartment window in Prague on December 20, 1997. Six months later the man who Glazar's testimony helped put behind bars, Kurt Franz, died of natural causes.

The destruction people can do to others is a great evil. Amidst the worst of these circumstances, however, there is something deeper happening, concealed inside the individuals themselves. The Nazis, driven by evil, and exhaustive in their efforts to abolish a distinct people group, consequently lost themselves, and in fact lost their own identity and became a people morally obsolete.

The Jews, even while heavily persecuted, resisted within Warsaw, at Treblinka, and in other cities and camps throughout Europe. This fight for survival and justice gained for them a remarkable authoritative presence, a presence that allowed them to bravely stand against the Nazi defendants' outright lies and blame-erasing tactics at the Nuremberg and Dusseldorf trials. It also empowered them to make a new life, often without relatives, starting completely over, and usually in a new land, where they knew no one. But they did it.

I wrote *Trains to Treblinka* to unveil an incredible resilience innate to the human spirit. This fountain, elucidated and empowered by divine presence, forever stands against impossible adversities, fights against the greatest of odds, and contains hope for even the slightest of victories, of light over darkness, and of good over evil. As David Brat encouraged Richard Glazar moments before the Treblinka revolt, "'Yea, though I walk through the valley of the shadow of death, I will fear no evil, for thou art with me…'"

THE END

Bibliography and

Chapter Notes

Arad, Yitzhak. *Belzec, Sobibor, Treblinka: The Operation Reinhard Death Camps*. Bloomington: Indiana University Press, 1987.

Bryant, Michael S. *Eyewitness to Genocide: The Operation Reinhard Death Camp Trials, 1955–1966*. Knoxville: The University of Tennessee Press, 2014.

Causey, Charles. *The Lion and the Lamb: The Holocaust Story of a Powerful Nazi Leader and a Dutch Resistance Worker*. Bloomington, IN: Westbow Press, a Division of Thomas Nelson and Zondervan, 2016.

Cesarani, David. *The Final Solution: The Fate of the Jews 1933–1949*. New York: St. Martin's Press, 2016.

Donat, Alexander. *The Death Camp Treblinka*. New York: Walden, 1979.

Gallagher, Hugh Gregory. *By Trust Betrayed: Patients, Physicians, and the License to Kill in the Third Reich*. New York: Henry Holt and Company, 1993.

Gerwarth, Robert. *Hitler's Hangman: The Life of Heydrich*. New Haven: Yale University Press, 2011.

Gilbert, G. M. *Nuremberg Diary*. New York: Da Capo Press, 1947.

Glazar, Richard. *Trap with a Green Fence: Survival in Treblinka*. Evanston: Northwestern University Press, 1995.

Grossman, Vasily. *The Hell of Treblinka*. Moscow, 1946.

155

Kopówka, Edward & Rytel-Andrianik, Pawel. *I Will Give Them an Everlasting Name*. Loreto Sisters Publishing House, 2011.

Longerich, Peter. *Heinrich Himmler*. New York: Oxford University Press, 2012.

Lubling, Yoram. *Twice Dead: Moshe Y. Lubling. The Ethics of Memory, and the Treblnika Revolt*. New York: Peter Lang Publishing, 2007.

Poprzeczny, Joseph. *Odilo Globocnik, Hitler's Man in the East*. Jefferson, NC: McFarland & Company, 2004.

Rajchman, Chil. *The Last Jew of Treblinka: A Memoir*. New York: Pegasus, 2011.

Reitlinger, Gerald. *The Final Solution: The Attempt to Exterminate the Jews of Europe, 1939–1945*. London: Sphere Books Limited, 1961.

Roseman, Mark. *The Wannsee Conference and the Final Solution: A Reconsideration*. New York: Metropolitan Books, 2002.

Segev, Tom. *The Seventh Million: The Israelis and the Holocaust*. New York: Owl Books, 1991.

Sereny, Gitta. *Into that Darkness: An Examination of Conscience*. New York: Vintage, 1974.

Shirer, William L. *The Rise and Fall of the Third Reich*. New York: Crest Books, 1959.

Smith, Mark S. *Treblinka Survivor: The Life and Death of Hershl Sperling*. Stroud, Gloucestershire: The History Press, 2010.

Snyder, Timothy. *Bloodlands: Europe Between Hitler and Stalin*. New York: Basic Books, 2010.

Treblinka Trial. *Benjamin Sagalowitz Archive: Documentation regarding the Treblinka Trial in Duesseldorf, 1960–1965*. YVA Item ID # 3689563.

Treiger, Karen I. *My Soul is Filled with Joy: A Holocaust Story*. Seattle: Stare Lipke Press, 2018.

Webb, Chris & Chocholaty, Michal. *The Treblinka Death Camp: History, Biographies, Remembrance*. Stuttgart: Ibidem Press, 2014.

Wiernik, Jankiel. *A Year in Treblinka: An Inmate Who Escaped Tells the Day to Day Facts of One Year of His Torturous Experiences*. New York: Normanby Press, 2015.

Willenberg, Samuel. *Surviving Treblinka*. Hoboken: Blackwell Publishers, 1989.

Wójcik, Michal. *Treblinka 43*. Kraków: Znak, 2018.

As the following sources are used frequently, they will be abbreviated as shown:

ARAD *The Operation Reinhard Death Camps*, Arad

EYE *Eyewitness to Genocide*, Bryant

CAMP *The Death Camp Treblinka*, Donat

TRAP *Trap with a Green Fence*, Glazar

INTO *Into that Darkness*, Sereny

PREFACE

1. The protagonists. There were certainly many intriguing Jewish workers to write about, such as Treblinka survivor Samuel Rajzman, who spent a year living in the woods after the revolt (CAMP 245), or Zev Kurland, who assisted Mentz at the *Lazarette* (INTO 246, TRAP 56), or Moshe Lubling, a revolt planner who sacrificed his own life to help others escape (TRAP 148). But in an effort not to overwhelm the reader, I consolidated most of the Jewish worker narrative to two young women from Poland (Bronka and Tchechia) and six Czech men who were central to the revolt (Hans, Karel, Richard, Robert, Rudi, and Zelo). The carpenter Jankiel Wiernik is also important to *Trains to Treblinka*, but he is not a dominant character. I also did not write about all the notorious guards who served there. One in particular, Ivan Marchenko (Ivan the Terrible), a Ukrainian guard, was known to torture people in the tube before they entered the gas chamber.

2. A spurious resource. I purposely decided not to consider the 1966 Jean-Francois Steiner book *Treblinka: The Revolt of an Extermination Camp* as source material for *Trains to Treblinka* because the book was republished as a novel. I also declined its use out of respect to Richard Glazar, who wrote a letter to Steiner in 1968 to protest Steiner's "completely phony" descriptions of Treblinka camp life. At one point Glazar told Steiner, "One could argue with you over almost every page of your book." At another point he stated, "And as for you, today, Jean, I know of another type of terrible human cowardice and weakness, namely when a person is unable to admit that his ideas fail to stand up to reality." Karel Unger and Samuel Rajzman agreed with Glazar. Once, Unger told Glazar, "That man (Steiner) must be repudiated." Samuel Rajzman wrote to Glazar, "This terrible book prevented me from sleeping for many a long night." Even Franz Suchomel, a Nazi guard, declared to Gitta Sereny that Steiner's book was just invention (INTO 206). In my opinion, the actual events at Treblinka were worse than anyone could fathom, so to contrive imaginative stories only serves to belittle those who truly lived them.

3. Description of Tchechia (ARAD 152, 323; INTO 195, 203–205; TRAP 100). "Tchechia Mandel was the only real red-blond in the camp," said Suchomel. In at least one source Tchechia Mandel is referred to as "Chesia Mendel" (Arad) or "Cescha" (Glazar), but the predominant spelling of her name is Tchechia Mandel. I do not know definitively if Bronka and Tchechia arrived on the same train. One source suggested that Bronka may not have arrived at Treblinka until January of '43, but her exact arrival date is unverifiable. It is assumed that all but a fraction of the steady workers were selected by the end of October, so it would be exceptional if Bronka arrived so late yet was chosen to be a worker. Glazar wrote about Tchechia, "She works in the German mess, and the few girls who are here look up to her the same way we looked up to Zelo."

4. Bronka Sukno (ARAD 151, EYE 111, INTO 192). She was deported to Treblinka from the Warsaw ghetto. "After about two hours there, Suchomel took me to the laundry where the Germans' clothing was washed and ironed. On the way Suchomel told me not to ask any questions, and to remember that I had neither heard nor seen a thing. The next day they

took me to the tailor's shop." –Bronka Sukno's testimony to the Israeli police, June 14, 1961. In some Shoah literature, Bronka Sukno's first name is spelled Broncha.

CHAPTER 1

1. Gisela Masarek. I am indebted to the Holocaust Historical Society for this name. I could find no Treblinka literature that named Rudi Masarek's young wife, but I felt *Trains to Treblinka* would not be complete without it. Consulting with the Holocaust Historical Society, they were not only able to retrieve Gisela's name, but provided her date of birth as well, April 18, 1923 (the same day of the year my father was born). Gisela was nineteen years old when she stepped off the train at Treblinka station. Rudi was twenty-nine.

2. Rudi and Hans (CAMP 283, INTO 182–183, TRAP 23)

3. Theresienstadt Ghetto (EYE 105)

4. One of the most deplorable aspects of the Holocaust were the cruel, ghastly train rides to the death camps. Many people died on their journey to Treblinka. Cattle cars, which could hold sixty to seventy people without luggage, would be crammed with between 100–150 people and all of their belongings. There was often panic and a fight to find fresh air to breathe. The floors were sometimes dusted with lime and chlorine by the Nazis, which burned the Jews' eyes and feet, and caused many to gag. Some trains arrived at Treblinka station filled with corpses of people who died of asphyxiation. The following is from Jakub Krzepicki regarding his journey from Warsaw to Treblinka: "…It is impossible to describe the tragic situation in our airless, closed freight car. It was one big toilet…the stink in the car was unbearable. People were defecating in all four corners." Abraham Goldfarb reported that in his train to Treblinka packed with 150 passengers, 135 died before the doors were opened (ARAD 100–101). To make matters worse, sometimes the guards would shoot into the cars for sport. From Warsaw to Treblinka the train ride should have taken approximately four hours, but many times it would take two full days. This gratuitous suffering was an evil almost as inconceivable as the gas chambers. The trains became for many a rolling chamber of death.

CHAPTER 2

1. Franz Stangl (CAMP 274, INTO 167–171, TRAP 46). The scene depicts Stangl witnessing Rudi's train arrive, which is a continuation from chapter 2. Chapter 3 departs this sequence and depicts Tchechia and Bronka's train, which came from Poland. Chapter 4 continues with the arrival of the Czech train. I hope this interchanging sequence adds dimension and is not confusing for the reader.

2. Stangl's contempt for his father's uniform (INTO 25). "His Dragoon uniform, always carefully brushed and pressed, hung in the wardrobe. I was so sick of it, I got to hate uniforms. I knew since I was very small, I don't remember exactly when, that my father hadn't really wanted me. I heard them talk. He thought I wasn't really his." For more detailed information on Stangl's personal life, see chapter 5, note #3.

3. Odilo Globocnik, chief of the extermination program (ARAD 34, EYE 3): Reitlinger, Gerald. *The Final Solution: The Attempt to Exterminate the Jews of Europe, 1939–1945*. London: Sphere Books Limited, 1961, 71. Snyder, Timothy. *Bloodlands: Europe Between Hitler and Stalin*. New York: Basic Books, 2010, 209. Globocnik was one of the earliest Nazis and had an enduring friendship with Himmler, which *earned* him the opportunity to prove himself in Poland. Himmler's nickname for Globocnik was "Globus," and they worked in concert to establish the Operation Reinhard death camps. Globocnik employed fear and intimidation on men like Stangl and Kurt Franz. He was captured on May 31, 1945 in the Austrian Alps, but unfortunately he was never brought to trial. Just like his mentor Himmler, Globus committed suicide by biting on a cyanide capsule moments before he was to be interrogated by the Allied army.

CHAPTER 3

1. The smell of death in this instance is partially from Camp 2, but at that time they were still burying corpses. It is also from the *Lazarette*, where they routinely burned bodies not too far from the unloading platform.

2. Bronka's selection (EYE 111, INTO 192). One account states that Bronka's older brother, who was already at the camp, asked Suchomel to select her. The account that aligns closer to the historical record, however, is taken from Bryant's *Eyewitness to Genocide*, which states that it was a friend

of one of her sisters who pleaded with Suchomel. Perhaps the prisoner lied about their relationship (calling himself Bronka's brother) to ensure Suchomel chose Bronka, so both stories may be accurate.

3. The city of Lemberg is the name in German; in Polish it is Lwow. After WWII it became Lviv, Ukraine.

CHAPTER 4

1. Rudi's arrival (CAMP 283). Donat's account says that Rudi arrived with not only his wife Gisela but also her mother, and Gisela's thirteen-year-old sister. All the women were sent immediately into the tube.

2. Hans Freund worried of his son having a cold (INTO 211–212)

3. The *Lazarette* (TRAP 13). This area was disguised to look like a medical clinic. It was actually a killing and burning center. When not disposing of bodies, Mentz was tasked to burn all the documents the Jews brought with them to Treblinka. Cesarani, David. *The Final Solution: The Fate of the Jews, 1933–1949*. New York: St. Martin's Press, 2016, 504.

4. Richard and Karel arrived at Treblinka on Saturday, October 10, 1942, (TRAP 5, 137).

5. *Kapos* and foremen. These terms were used interchangeably at the camp, but *kapo* was a name a little more formal. Toward the beginning the *kapos* were harsher with their coworkers; this was partially coerced by the Nazis, though some did it for sport. Over time many of the *kapos* at Treblinka became revolt conspirators, and they were able to weed out the informers.

CHAPTER 5

1. Stangl's recollection of arriving at Treblinka and his encounter with Globocnik (INTO 157–160). *"It was Dante's Inferno!"*

2. The first *kommandant* of Treblinka was Dr. Irmfried Eberl. He notified the commissar of the Warsaw ghetto that Treblinka would be ready for operation on July 11, 1942. The first transport of Jews from Warsaw arrived on July 23, 1942. The truth was that Treblinka was not prepared under his leadership. Eberl was relieved one month later. He survived the

war and was arrested in January 1948. He committed suicide a few weeks later to avoid trial (CAMP 274).

3. Stangl's family. Franz Stangl and Theresa Eidenbock were married October 7, 1935 and they had three daughters before the end of WWII; Brigitte (born July 7, 1936 and called "Gitta"), Renate (February 17, 1937), and Isolde (January 5, 1944). In what might be considered an ironic exchange of fate, until the day of his death Stangl felt that his capture on February 28, 1967 was the result of an informant, his estranged son-in-law Herbert Havel (married to Renate). Though the story about Havel's role does not have a lot of supporting evidence (Sereny), it did take Nazi hunter Simon Wiesenthal three years to find Stangl, and he must have had a break from someone who knew Stangl's current residence.

CHAPTER 6

1. The nightly suicides. Wiernik reported, "Such suicides occurred at the rate of 15 to 20 a day." Wiernik, Jankiel. *A Year in Treblinka: An Inmate Who Escaped Tells the Day to Day Facts of One Year of His Torturous Experiences*. New York: Normanby Press, 2015, Ch. 7.

2. Karel and Richard (INTO 182)

3. The Doll, Kiewe, and Miete (CAMP 276–278, TRAP 46–47), and virtually every resource describing Treblinka

4. The guards as sadists (INTO 188)

5. David Brat (TRAP 21, 49)

6. For more information on the escape attempts, see chapter 10, note #4.

7. Camp elder Galewski (CAMP 215). There is much written on Galewski regarding his help overseeing the workers and his support for the revolt. Sometimes his name is misspelled by the survivors, such as by Stanislaw Kon in his writing *Revolt in Treblinka and the Liquidation of the Camp*. Kon spelled the camp elder's name as Gralewski. There is also no historic consensus on his first name. Some say it must be Alfred, others Marceli. Possibly his full name was Alfred Marceli Galewski and he predominantly went by his middle name (which contributed to the source of confusion among sources).

8. The motor utilized to create diesel exhaust fumes for the gas chamber was the engine of a Russian T-34 tank. It had been captured from the Russians, taken apart, and installed at Treblinka. Globocnik preferred carbon monoxide poisoning to Zyklon B (hydrogen cyanide), which was used at Auschwitz-Birkenau, possibly because of the increased suffering. With the crystal pellets of Zyklon B its victims were killed after just a few breaths; with diesel exhaust it took twenty-five to thirty-five minutes (Camp 2 survivor Eliahu Rosenberg testimony). The comparative results were staggering; in Zyklon B chambers people died standing up, nearly in the same position as when they had entered, like they were frozen. With diesel exhaust people had time and energy to attempt to fight for air. The chambers would be filled with an entangled mound of individuals where the stronger ones had climbed to the top in a struggle for oxygen, a grisly display of the survival of the fittest. The workers at Camp 2 had to witness these images every time the door opened to the chamber. The Treblinka trial lead state prosecutor, Alfred Spiess, discussed this in an interview with the *Westdeutscher Rundfunk* television network, and he referenced the Gerstein Report.

9. The story of the ham is credited to Joe Siedlecki (INTO 190).

CHAPTER 7
1. Rudi's father in the shirt business (INTO 182). "His family had owned one of the most exclusive men's shirt shops in Prague."

2. Dr. Chorazycki (CAMP 280–281, INTO 205–206, TRAP 100). His name is also referred to as Choronzycki (Sereny) or Chorandzicki (Bryant).

3. In Glazar's book *Trap with a Green Fence*, there is a worker named Rybak who managed the sick bay. It seems he was Dr. Chorazycki's replacement, though the timing for his service is varied in key Treblinka source material.

CHAPTER 8
1. Franz Stangl daily life (INTO 168–171)

2. Christian Wirth (CAMP 272–273). Every description of this Nazi is vile. After his work with the German euthanasia program in the late '30s, he worked at Chelmno (an early, pre-Operation Reinhard death camp), then became the first Belzec *kommandant*. Wirth was instrumental in the

transition from death vans (Chelmno) to death chambers (Belzec), where, instead of using the back of a vehicle, carbon monoxide from diesel fumes was pumped into a building with doors that could seal, thus greatly magnifying their ability for mass extinction. This is Wirth's historical marker. Stangl described Wirth as having awful verbal crudity. Stangl's friend Michel (at Sobibor) stated that Wirth acted like a lunatic and would whip his own men (ARAD 233, INTO 113–114). Wirth was killed in combat in the Trieste region on May 26, 1944. Stangl saw Wirth's dead body and told Sereny that he was killed by his own men, Ibid. 262.

3. The gold Jews. The gold Jews, or *goldjuden*, were a specialized group of workers skilled in currencies, jewels, and precious metals. They assisted not only with the gold arriving from the transports but also the gold extracted from the teeth of the victims at Camp 2. Occasionally they would make requested items into gold for the SS.

CHAPTER 9

1. Zelo (CAMP 279, INTO 182–183, TRAP 22–23). Yitzhak Arad spelled his name Zialo. Gitta Sereny spelled his name Zhelo. I decided to throw in my lot with Richard Glazar, the man who knew Zelo best.

2. Revolt planning, Ibid. 69–72. There were multiple survivors who credited Zelo with strong leadership for the revolt, yet in my research I found testimony of others who had a central role. It is hard to know the precise nature of everyone who helped because in some instances the planning was purposely decentralized as a mask for suspected informers. One of the other strong leaders was Moshe Y. Lubling, and for learning this fact I am indebted to his grandson's work, *Twice Dead: Moshe Y. Lubling. The Ethics of Memory, and the Treblnika Revolt*. New York: Peter Lang Publishing, 2007. Dr. Yoram Lubling used prima facie source material to place his grandfather at the center of the revolt planning (which the earliest Treblinka testimonies attested and had never been rebutted, just ignored). His book also exposed some of the flaws in early Holocaust research, perpetuating confusion even today. Although many of the stories of revolt leadership are fragmented, most mention Zelo. "The title of chief of staff must be given to Zelo," wrote Stanislaw Kon (CAMP 226). Dr. Chorazycki was certainly the center of gravity for appropriating the currency and gold,

and also purchasing items for the revolt, but Zelo was the leader of the military planning.

3. The time of "lights-out" varied at the different death camps. Lights-out usually occurred at 2100 hours at Treblinka, 2200 hours at Sobibor, and a half an hour after nightfall at Belzec (ARAD 255). "At nine o'clock all candles must be put out and everyone must be in his bed," wrote Glazar (TRAP 27).

CHAPTER 10

1. Galewski (CAMP 281–282, TRAP 57). "All of us had great respect for Galewski" (INTO 183).

2. Jankiel Wiernik (CAMP 147–148). Also see Wiernik's book *A Year in Treblinka: An Inmate Who Escaped Tells the Day to Day Facts of One Year of His Torturous Experiences*. New York: Normanby Press, 2015.

3. Whippings of escaped men (TRAP 41)

4. Escape attempts. Successful escapes prior to the revolt were critically important to the Jewish leaders in Warsaw, because some of the men returned to the ghetto and reported on the veracity of Treblinka being a death camp. A few of the men who escaped were actually sent back. Samuel Rajzman told a remarkable story about a man who escaped from Treblinka twice but was deported to Treblinka thrice. He was helpful to the Warsaw revolt planners in exchanging information, and he was helpful to those stuck in Treblinka because he delivered messages back and forth. It was not his intent to ever return to Treblinka after his first escape, just his misfortune. Rajzman said the man died in the uprising (CAMP 235).

CHAPTER 11

1. The Doll (CAMP 276–277, TRAP 47). Kurt Franz was the most notorious of the SS guards at the camp, and it seems as though every person who passed through Treblinka possessed wicked stories about the Doll… except for Sam Goldberg. As described in Karen Treiger's recent book, her father-in-law Sam became the Doll's preferred prisoner and the Doll went out of his way to help Sam stay alive. This is an aberration to what others testified about Franz, but it aligns with the Czech's protégé theory. Treiger's book is a great read, filled with impactful, reflective commentary.

Treiger, Karen I. *My Soul is Filled with Joy: A Holocaust Story*. Seattle: Stare Lipke Press, 2018.

2. The Doll's atrocities (EYE 78–82, INTO 202). Rajchman, Chil. *The Last Jew of Treblinka: A Memoir*. New York: Pegasus, 2011, 83. Smith, Mark S. *Treblinka Survivor: The Life and Death of Hershl Sperling*. Stroud, Gloucestershire: The History Press, 2010, 102.

3. The Doll whips a man to death (TRAP 41)

4. Bari the dog (EYE 108). Webb, Chris & Chocholaty, Michal. *The Treblinka Death Camp: History, Biographies, Remembrance*. Stuttgart: Ibidem Press, 2014. 116. Bari, a mongrel dog the size of a calf, is mentioned in nearly all Camp 1 testaments. Though the phrase "Boy, sic the dog!" seems backward, Kurt Franz used the phrase as an intentional derogatory inversion to humiliate his victims. After his time at Treblinka, Bari was known to be docile.

5. "You Jews started the war" (CAMP 240).

CHAPTER 12
1. Richard Glazar, the son of a financial consultant (INTO 172)

2. *Kapo* Rakowski. "He is the biggest speculator in the entire camp, a glutton, a boozer, a bellyacher. And he's not looking out for anyone but himself," wrote Richard Glazar (TRAP 99).

3. Selections of traitors, Ibid. 35–36

4. Tchechia and Rakowski. "Then there was Tchechia. She was in love with Rakowski, the former camp elder. And he, they said, was in love with her" (INTO 195, TRAP 100).

CHAPTER 13
1. Edek, Ibid. 30. Glazar explained Edek's appearance at Treblinka: "His parents and siblings were sent into the pipeline immediately after their arrival. They had not played any musical instrument."

2. The nighttime resistance (CAMP 190–191). Smith, Mark S. *Treblinka Survivor: The Life and Death of Hershl Sperling*. Stroud, Gloucestershire: The History Press, 2010, 115.

3. The whippings of Kurt Franz (INTO 202). Joe Siedlecki told Gitta Sereny, "He'd give them fifty strokes. They'd be dead at the end. He'd be half dead himself, but he'd beat and beat."

4. David and Richard's conversation about the difference in treatment of Warsaw's Jews compared to Czech Jews (TRAP 65).

5. December fires and Edek playing "*Eli, Eli*" (INTO 193). Glazar told Sereny the fires started in December. In his own book there is a reference to the fires in November (TRAP 29).

CHAPTER 14

1. Stangl and construction work (INTO 200)

2. The revolt known as plan H (TRAP 69–70)

3. Samuel Willenberg. Mr. Willenberg was nineteen years old when he arrived at Treblinka in October 1942. He was the last known survivor of the revolt and died on February 19, 2016 at the age of ninety-three. His daughter Orit Willenberg-Giladi was the architect who designed the Israeli embassy in Berlin. Mr. Willenberg's memoir a great contribution to Holocaust history. Willenberg, Samuel. *Surviving Treblinka*. Hoboken: Blackwell Publishers, 1989. At his funeral, Israeli president Reuven Rivlin described him as "a symbol for an entire generation of heroic Holocaust survivors." There is an outstanding film made about Willenberg's life called *Treblinka's Last Witness*, produced by Alan Tomlinson.

4. Standa Lichtblau. A professional mechanic by trade from Moravian Ostrow, Standa was also a Czech and became a useful coconspirator of the revolt planners. Glazar declared that Standa's work blowing up the gas tank might have been the most important part of the revolt (TRAP 72, 148, also in INTO 246).

5. Dropping like flies to typhus (TRAP 72)

CHAPTER 15

1. Suchomel working with T4 (INTO 56–57)

2. Bronka's story about Suchomel (EYE 111). This was not the only death attributed to Suchomel. At the Dusseldorf trial another Treblinka survivor,

Sigmund Strawczynski, testified that Suchomel shot a small child as it walked crying to the gas chamber with its mother, Ibid. 118.

CHAPTER 16

1. Zelo and Adasch transferring to Camp 2 (INTO 210–211, TRAP 80–82)

2. Hans Freund: "We aren't human beings anymore!" (INTO 211, TRAP 82). The long-haired man from religion class refers to the Old Testament figure of Samson from the book of Judges.

3. Trains from Bulgaria, feasting, and workers fighting (INTO 213, TRAP 94–95)

CHAPTER 17

1. The hands of the clock on the side of the tower. Some references state six and one resource states three. I used the predominant testimony. "Up on the gable there is an oversized clock face. Its hands always show six o'clock" (TRAP 141). From Smith, Mark S. *Treblinka Survivor: The Life and Death of Hershl Sperling.* Stroud, Gloucestershire: The History Press, 2010, 113," A painted clock with numerals permanently reading six o'clock adorned its façade." Also, Samuel Willenberg discussed the clock during an interview with his wife Ada that is in the Yad Vashem library, https://www. yadvashem.org/articles/interviews/willenberg.html.

2. Trains arriving with corpses, Wiernik, Jankiel. *A Year in Treblinka: An Inmate Who Escaped Tells the Day to Day Facts of One Year of His Torturous Experiences.* New York: Normanby Press, 2015, Ch. 3.

CHAPTER 18

1. Dr. Chorazycki's death (INTO 206, TRAP 101–102)

2. The story about the gold Jews (INTO 206). For more information on the gold Jews, see chapter 8, Note #3.

3. Rakowski's fate (TRAP 113)

4. The Doll's speech about Rakowski (CAMP 217)

CHAPTER 19

1. Gas chambers, Rajchman, Chil. *The Last Jew of Treblinka: A Memoir*. New York: Pegasus, 2011, 65.

2. *"Ivan, water!"* (TRAP 12). This was a reference to Ivan Marchenko (Ivan the Terrible). An interesting case, Ivan Demjanjuk, a Ukrainian guard, was thought to be Ivan the Terrible from Treblinka and was convicted on April 18, 1988 then sentenced to death by hanging. While on death row, on July 29, 1993, a five-judge panel of the Israeli Supreme Court overturned the conviction on appeal. New documents opened up after the fall of the Berlin Wall based on the testimony of twenty-three guards who were convicted of war crimes in the Soviet Union showed that it was Ivan Marchenko, not Ivan Demjanjuk, who was Ivan the Terrible. However, on May 12, 2011, at the age of ninety-one, Demjanjuk *was* convicted of accessory to murder of 27,900 Jews at Sobibor, where he worked as a guard. He was sentenced to five years in prison but died within a year of his conviction.

3. Camp 2 work, Rajchman, Chil. *The Last Jew of Treblinka: A Memoir*. New York: Pegasus, 2011, 47–51. Also, it is discussed in detail in Wiernik's book *A Year in Treblinka: An Inmate Who Escaped Tells the Day to Day Facts of One Year of His Torturous Experiences*. New York: Normanby Press, 2015.

CHAPTER 20

1. The Doll's concert plans (TRAP 122–125)

2. Arthur Gold (ARAD 252, 281; CAMP 306; TRAP 122). Snyder, Timothy. *Bloodlands: Europe Between Hitler and Stalin*. New York: Basic Books, 2010. 269.

3. There was also an orchestra in Camp 2, written about by survivor Jerzy Rajgrodzki (ARAD 283), Webb, Chris & Chocholaty, Michal. *The Treblinka Death Camp: History, Biographies, Remembrance*. Stuttgart: Ibidem Press, 2014. 112.

CHAPTER 21

1. Exchanging money for weapons with the peasants (CAMP 215). The camouflage patrol who went into the woods to bring back branches were

given license to wander away a little bit, and this was when the transaction would take place. It was Tanhum Grinberg who chronicled this story about peasants holding up fingers for how much money they wanted in exchange for a pistol. In a bewildering twist of fate, Grinberg survived the revolt and testified at Dusseldorf, but then was killed in an automobile accident in 1976. Glazar confirmed the speculating with the peasants while with the camouflage unit (TRAP 127–132).

2. Edek, the lock, and the grenades, Ibid. 109–110. Smith, Mark S. *Treblinka Survivor: The Life and Death of Hershl Sperling*. Stroud, Gloucestershire: The History Press, 2010, 122.

CHAPTER 22

1. The need to burn the bodies, Wiernik, Jankiel. *A Year in Treblinka: An Inmate Who Escaped Tells the Day to Day Facts of One Year of His Torturous Experiences*. New York: Normanby Press, 2015, Ch. 9.

2. The Katyn forest massacre, Smith, Mark S. *Treblinka Survivor: The Life and Death of Hershl Sperling*. Stroud, Gloucestershire: The History Press, 2010, 120.

3. The Artist. He was described by all those who escaped from Camp 2 and wrote about their experience. His actual name was most likely Herbert Floss, brought in to help with the disposal of the bodies after Himmler's visit (EYE 79).

CHAPTER 23

1. Confrontation of Stangl and Tchechia (INTO 203–204)

2. One thought-provoking part of this story is that Stangl did not remember Tchechia's name. In fact, he could not remember any of the Jewish names except for a Viennese man named Blau, whom he spoiled. And Blau, in quid pro quo, became a Nazi loyalist and informer, Ibid. 207–209. It was Suchomel who identified Tchechia as the girl Stangl spoke about.

CHAPTER 24

1. Cleaning the pits, Rajchman, Chil. *The Last Jew of Treblinka: A Memoir*. New York: Pegasus, 2011, 91.

2. Over sixty thousand bodies burning, Ibid. 91–92. Mr. Rajchman put the number much higher, at nearly a quarter of a million bodies. A trial transcript stated that at least one of the pits contained no less than eighty thousand corpses (CAMP 301). This figure in no way contradicts Mr. Rajchman's account; it verifies the magnitude of the exhumation work. At the second Treblinka trial Stangl told prosecutor Alfred Spiess that there were mass graves with one hundred thousand bodies in them.

3. The work of exhumation and the story of the women from Warsaw, Wiernik, Jankiel. *A Year in Treblinka: An Inmate Who Escaped Tells the Day to Day Facts of One Year of His Torturous Experiences.* New York: Normanby Press, 2015. Ch. 10. "Time and time again children were snatched from their mother's arms and tossed into the flames alive, while their tormentors laughed, urging the mothers to be brave and jump into the fire after their children and mocking the women for being cowards."

4. Carpenter Jankiel Wiernik and Chil Rajchman are the two chief sources on information about Camp 2. Sonia Lewkowicz is another source. Unfortunately Zelo was not able to write about it.

CHAPTER 25

1. Camouflage unit (INTO 220–221)

2. Paulinka (ARAD 152, INTO 247)

CHAPTER 26

1. Revolt day, August 2, 1943. Interestingly Reitlinger had the date wrong in his book and mistakenly named September 2, 1943 as the day of the uprising. This is the only source I have found with that error. Reitlinger, Gerald. *The Final Solution: The Attempt to Exterminate the Jews of Europe, 1939–1945.* London: Sphere Books Limited, 1961, 152.

2. "*Ha-yom, ha-yom!*" ("The day, the day!") Rajchman, Chil. *The Last Jew of Treblinka: A Memoir.* New York: Pegasus, 2011, 126.

3. Richard Glazar, "Not a cloud in the sky…" (TRAP 140).

4. David Brat tells Richard the verse about the shadow of death, Ibid. 139. The full verse is, "*Yea, though I walk through the valley of the shadow of death, I*

will fear no evil: for thou art with me; thy rod and thy staff they comfort me" (Psalm 23:4, KJV).

5. Kurt "Kiewe" Kuttner was wounded but did not actually die that day.

CHAPTER 27

1. The uprising (ARAD 334–343, CAMP 220–223, INTO 236–240, TRAP 138–146). Smith, Mark S. *Treblinka Survivor: The Life and Death of Hershl Sperling*. Stroud, Gloucestershire: The History Press, 2010, 130–144.

2. One of the main objectives of the revolt was to kill as many of the SS as possible. Unfortunately this goal was not accomplished. As mentioned above, even though Kiewe and Mentz were fired upon, they somehow survived with minor wounds. Kiewe lived for another twenty-one years and Mentz lived until 1978.

3. The fate of Paulinka (INTO 247)

CHAPTER 28

1. Eight hundred meters of a flower-lined street, Ibid. 239

2. Stangl's pride in his creation. Alfred Spiess reported that there were no official maps of Treblinka, not even a sketch. The court had to create a map based on witness testimony and the statements of the accused. Then later, in 1970, when Stangl was extradited to West Germany, Spiess showed the map to Stangl to see what he thought of it, since Stangl was the man who designed the camp to his perfection. Spiess reported that Stangl studied it for almost fifteen minutes, then looked up with surprise and admiration and said, "Mr. Prosecutor, the sketch is absolutely correct!"

3. Galewski's fate. Smith, Mark S. *Treblinka Survivor: The Life and Death of Hershl Sperling*. Stroud, Gloucestershire: The History Press, 2010, 134.

4. Bronka Sukno's escape is truly miraculous. Out of the twenty-five women at the camp, there were only four or five women who escaped from Treblinka that day, and only three who survived the war (the other two women were Sonia Grabinski and Sonia Lewkowicz). The fact that they survived the initial screening and selection process, the months of terror while living at the camp, the revolt, the rest of the war, then

living long enough to testify against the Nazi guards in the '60s is nearly unfathomable.

5. Another note about the women who escaped from Treblinka. In the book *Into That Darkness*, Gitta Sereny described a woman with the fictitious name of "Sabina," who was the girlfriend of *Kapo* Kuba and was sent up to Camp 2 by Kuttner because of their forbidden relationship (INTO 205). It could be that this "Sabina" was Sonia Lewkowicz, who was forced to leave Camp 1 and work at Camp 2 on March 5, 1943. Perhaps because there was another Sonia (Grabinski), Sonia Lewkowicz took the nickname of Sabina while at the camp. Or another possibility is that Sereny purposefully protected her reputation with a pseudonym since Lewkowicz was still alive when Sereny published her book in 1974. Richard Glazar wrote a letter to Sereny describing how *Kapo* Kuba was a barracks elder and a known informer (INTO 240). A snippet of the Fedorenko trial transcripts with the Sonia Lewkowicz portion of testimony is available online at: http://www.holocaustresearchproject.org/survivor/sonialewkowicz.html. Sonia Lewkowicz was the sole revolt escapee of the women who worked at Camp 2. Ms. Lewkowicz died in 2006.

6. The end of the revolt (INTO 247)

CHAPTER 29
1. Karel and Richard's escape (TRAP 146–150). "Look, this is a good sign. How do believers put it: the hand of the Lord is opened?" Ibid. 149.

2. These two young men were both twenty-one when they arrived at Treblinka in 1942 (INTO 180).

CHAPTER 30
1. Stangl and Globocnik, Ibid. 249. For more information on Globocnik, see chapter 2, note #3.

2. Shipping Treblinka survivors to Sobibor. Franciszek Zabecki, the rail-traffic controller, reported that it was October 20, 1943 when five railway cars left Treblinka for Sobibor with most of the residual Jewish workers. Immediately after the revolt Stangl gave the order that the remaining workers were not to be executed. Yet as soon as Stangl was reassigned, the Jews

were killed either at Treblinka or Sobibor. At Sobibor, the Treblinka Jews arrived one week after the Sobibor uprising (which is another fascinating story), and they were tasked with dismantling the buildings. Himmler had ordered Globocnik to dissolve this Operation Reinhard death camp immediately after the Sobibor revolt (October 14, 1943) in an effort to mask it from the public. Sobibor trial transcripts report that in late November all of the remaining Jews (some from both Treblinka and Sobibor) were taken to Camp 3, forced to lie down side by side on the grilling racks, then shot.

3. Killing the remaining Jews at Treblinka (ARAD 429, CAMP 315–316). Arad and other sources stated that just two females remained at the end (based on the Treblinka trial), but Suchomel (whose memory seemed flawless) told Sereny that there were three women left (INTO 250). Arad draws his account from the trial testimonies of Willi Mentz and Albert Rum but I gave precedence to Suchomel.

4. Tchechia's fate, Ibid. 195

POSTSCRIPT

1. The Dusseldorf trial. The Nuremberg trials and the Dusseldorf trial are helpful in a discussion of universal law and absolute truth. There had to be a type of law that represented civilized thought and superseded national law, whereby these defendants could be charged with crimes against humanity. At Nuremberg, a unique international war crimes court was created to deal with these crimes and render justice to the perpetrators of evil. The Nazis conducted business according to the laws of their country, and that was their defense. For the first time in history an international court formed to decree that there is a higher law—universal adherences to which all mankind are subject. Equality, decency, respect for other persons…all attributes of a fair and just society that constitute an authority that is absolute. National laws do not necessarily represent justice, but they do represent power. And Hitler wielded laws to execute and powerfully spread his evil will. For those who would propose that there is no absolute truth, then what should we have done with the Nazi war crimes defendants? Where do we even get this idea of what is just and what is unjust? Indeed, even the desire for retribution comes from something innate in us

that betokens an absolute truth, and universal laws are the instruments by which we expect our courts to rule.

2. Abraham Kolski story (EYE 116). I thank the author of *Eyewitness to Genocide*, Michael S. Bryant, for his very detailed research explaining the death-camp workers' testimonies at the Operation Reinhard trials.

3. Here are the September 3rd verdicts:

Kurt Franz (the Doll)	Life imprisonment
Otto Horn	Acquitted
Kurt Kuttner (Kiewe)	Died before trial
Erwin Lambert	Four years
Heinrich Matthes	Life imprisonment
Willi Mentz	Life imprisonment
August Miete	Life imprisonment
Gustav Munzberger	Twelve years
Albert Rum	Three years
Otto Stadie	Six years
Franz Stangl	Life imprisonment (at a later trial)
Franz Suchomel	Seven years

Although the verdicts at the Treblinka trial far outshined the Belzec trial (with its one conviction of four and a half years), the majority of SS men and Ukrainian guards who served at Treblinka were never brought to trial.

4. Kurt Franz, the best years of my life (CAMP 277). Interestingly, during the trial it seemed that Kurt Franz (the Doll) was more concerned about some of the *particular* crimes attributed to him rather than his all-embracing complicity with the magnitude of incriminating evidence from Treblinka. It would be a fascinating study for psychiatrists to see why one death of an infant, or of the camp doctor, was an assault on Franz's conscience more than the murder in concert of hundreds of thousands. It could be that these individual events somehow made the crime real to him; that he would be guilty of an offense that demanded punishment. In effect, one or two deaths—attested to by survivors—would put blood on his innocent hands (his perspective). For the first time in his life the light of truth

attempted to pierce the impenetrable black abyss of his heart, whereby Franz could have addressed his moral corruption. But it did not happen. He supposed it would have commenced an unmasking too unbearable for him to endure. Before the trial, Franz spoke of the atrocities as if he was describing fiction—something impossible for him to have had any responsibility. At the trial, when questioned on matters whereby the eyewitness evidence unquestionably connected him to murder, it was at this point if he had admitted something then he would have had to truly *feel* for the victims. However, all through the trial the victims remained numbers, not names, and simply a consequence of Nazi war crimes, not his own. His alarming separation of actions with corresponding feelings remained intact. His perversion was complete.

5. When trying to decide on the number of deaths at Treblinka, survivor Samuel Rajzman told Alexander Donat that he was present when the Nazis celebrated their one-millionth victim, and it was long before operations were over (CAMP 14). Richard Glazar believed that Treblinka had executed one million people by the end of March 1943, four full months before the revolt (INTO 213–214). This is why I think Franciszek Zabecki might be the closest to the truth, with 1.2 million, Ibid. 250.

6. Another note on the numbers, in Richard Glazar's letter to Steiner (Yad Vashem Archives) he wrote that one day alone they processed eighteen thousand prisoners through the tube. If the Nazis murdered an average of one-third of that number for only half of the days of just one year (the camp was "active" for sixteen months), it would put the number around 1.1 million, the same number of people who perished at Auschwitz. In Yitzhak Arad's book *The Operation Reinhard Death Camps*, he reported that in just one five-week period of July 23, 1942 to August 28, 1942, 312,500 were killed at Treblinka (ARAD 124). Cesarani repeated this number in his tome and stated that two hundred thousand were specifically from Warsaw. Cesarani, David. *The Final Solution: The Fate of the Jews, 1933–1949*. New York: St. Martin's Press, 2016, 507.

7. Sixty-seven survivors. According to Donat there were actually eighty-six survivors (and the Muzeum Treblinka in Poland reiterated Donat's number). Some online sources even report ninety-seven survivors. The reason

my number is lower is because I only include those who survived the war due to the revolt. Donat and others include those who had escaped previously (in the months leading up to the revolt, such as Abraham Bomba), thus the higher number.

8. Absences of witnesses at Belzec (EYE 123)

9. Albert Speer was one of Hitler's closest confidantes. His official title was Reich Minister of Armaments and War Production.

10. David Brat saying that Richard must survive (INTO 181)

11. Stangl's guilt and death, Ibid. 364–5

12. Kurt Franz. The attorney for Franz at Dusseldorf did not allow him to testify, but in the mid-nineties Franz gave a rare post-prison interview. He maintained that when he arrived at Belzec (his first death-camp assignment), he did not know what was going to happen, and did not know why they were digging pits. He claimed that he was outraged at the gassings and pleaded for a new assignment. He stated that he was still really mad at Suchomel for incriminating him at the trial. At the end of the interview he was asked repeatedly why the Jews were murdered and if they had committed any crime deserving punishment. He said that he did not believe that they had, then declared that he personally did not have any trouble with Jews, and that two of his friends were Jews. The gist of the interview is that Franz continued to deflect his role and responsibility, and never owned up to the fact that he had materially participated in the Holocaust. It was as if the whole mess was an inconvenience to *his* life alone. From Franz's own words: "If I knew then, what was in store for me, when I transferred from the armed forces to the SS, I would have never joined the SS. Just because I can't bear what I have experienced, this Treblinka and this Belzec."

13. Karl Ludwig (ARAD 245, INTO 188). Joe Siedlecki: "There was an SS man, Karl Ludwig. He was a good man. If I would meet him today I would give him everything he might need." Ada Lichtman (on Ludwig): "More than once he took people from the lines. In this way he saved two doctors." Also, Jankiel Wiernik reported that an SS man at Treblinka, Erwin Herman Lambert, frequently brought him food from the German kitchen.

14. Rapaport and his pregnant wife (EYE 104–105)

15. Abraham Bomba. The United States Holocaust Memorial Museum has videos of Bomba describing his experiences at Treblinka. He was transported to Treblinka on September 25, 1942. An amazingly heroic feat, Bomba escaped with two other men months before the revolt (ARAD 308).

16. Hershl Sperling's death, Smith, Mark S. *Treblinka Survivor: The Life and Death of Hershl Sperling*. Stroud, Gloucestershire: The History Press, 2010, 11–19. Sperling departed his home to take his life on Tuesday, September 26, 1989, exactly forty-seven years after he arrived at Treblinka. He had survived seven Nazi concentration camps.

17. Richard Glazar's death. Glazar's testimony provided incontrovertible proof of Holocaust death camps, yet Richard somehow couldn't reconcile his own existence. He committed suicide on December 20, 1997. At the conclusion of his book, the date is May 8, 1945, which is Victory Europe Day and Glazar wrote about the war being over: "As soon as the sun sets everyone rips the blackout shades out of the windows. Their own light will stream out into this new sky. From beyond the Rhine one of the searchlights is sweeping back and forth across the sky from one end to the other, and I am fascinated. I know what the boy beyond the horizon is signaling to the whole world: 'I will not be killed—I will not be slaughtered—I will live—love—live.'" Glazar took his own life five years after his book *Trap with a Green Fence* was published.

18. The full verse of what David Brat shared with Glazar: "*Yea, though I walk through the valley of the shadow of death, I will fear no evil: for thou art with me; thy rod and thy staff they comfort me*" (Psalm 23:4, KJV).

QUESTIONS FOR CLASSROOM STUDENTS AND BOOK CLUBS

1. What was *Kommandant* Franz Stangl's motivation for telling his staff not to treat the workers so harshly? Do you think he was an effective leader?

2. What leadership traits did Tchechia display even though she was not in an official leadership role?

3. What was it about Zelo that made him an effective leader? How did he use his leadership to inspire others?

4. In the discussion between Bronka and Rudi about their supervisor Suchomel on whether he was a kind man or not, would you agree more with Bronka or with Rudi?

5. Why was the loss of Zelo so impactful to the revolt organizers in Camp 1? How did they display their frustration?

6. How did the gold Jews survive their interrogation from the Doll the day Dr. Chorazycki died? What lesson can be gained from them, if any?

7. Was it helpful to the revolt organizers for Zelo to be transferred to Camp 2? Why, or why not?

8. Did any of the Nazi guards have good qualities? Is it even possible to think in those terms considering their brutality? Why, or why not?

9. How would you describe Tchechia's philosophy in life? How could it be advantageous or disadvantageous in a place like Treblinka?

10. As explained in this book, sometimes the Jewish workers would have sympathizers (those loyal to the Nazis who were informers) dealt with. Do you think this clandestine behavior of the workers was ethical in this circumstance? How is it different from the killings the Nazis were performing?

11. What was Jankiel Wiernik's role? How was he helpful to the revolt effort? Could the revolt have been pulled off without him? Why, or why not?

12. How did camp elder Galewski contribute toward the revolt? Was he an effective leader?

13. How did Tchechia handle herself during the revolt compared to Bronka?

14. When Stangl departed Treblinka he decided to shake hands with the workers. Was this appropriate? Why do you think he did so?

15. Who was your favorite character?

16. What do you think is the main lesson of Treblinka?

ACKNOWLEDGEMENTS

Special thanks to

The Documentation Center of Austrian Resistance
The Holocaust Historical Society, the United Kingdom
The Museum of Jewish Heritage, New York
The Museum of Struggle and Martyrdom in Treblinka, Poland
The United States Holocaust Memorial Museum, Washington D.C.
Yad Vashem (Document Archives and the Shoah Victims' Names
Database)

First, I thank the various authors who supplied the above references. Without the careful work documenting survivors' experiences (along with the trial transcripts), we would have never known the truth about Treblinka. I also extend a warm thank you to Rabbi Bonnie Koppell for her eloquent foreword. We have been friends and professional colleagues for many years and I greatly appreciate her partnering with me on this project.

I am very grateful to the Documentation Center of Austrian Resistance in Vienna, specifically Dr. Elisabeth Klamper, for authorizing the use of the cover photo. I thank the Museum of Jewish Heritage, specifically Elizabeth Edelstein, for her warm reception and eager help to assist with remaining questions I had about Treblinka. I also thank the Treblinka Museum director, Edward Kopówka, for his hospitality when I performed my on-site research in Poland. He was very helpful with instructing me on the latest research at Treblinka and was receptive to my work. Also, a special thanks to Chris Webb at the Holocaust Historical Society in London for his persistent responsiveness, and to the librarians and reference technicians at USHMM and Yad Vashem for their professionalism in providing requested information.

Next, I thank my kind and patient editor Vicki Zimmer for her hours of tedious sentence reconstructing. She also edited *The Lion and the Lamb* and I am grateful for her superb work on both projects. Vicki and her husband Mark are two of my closest friends from college, and they are wonderful people.

A warm thank you to Henry Foster, my friend and mentor in Columbia, SC, who graciously provided a painting for this book. A special thanks to Lauri and Madison Causey for reading an early version of the manuscript and offering constructive feedback. Lauri also performed some helpful editing for me along the way. She is amazing. Thanks to Todd Canfield for his friendship and hospitality over the final months before publication. Thank you Elm Hill team for your efforts in making Trains to Treblinka a reality for seeing my vision for *Trains to Treblinka*. Thank you to Julia Marie Edeler-Slinker for her help with German translation. Thank you to my beta readers (Janice Bertilson, Alan Cole, Virginia Emery, Beth Funk, Mark Jenkins, Cindy Rietema, and Joanne Teasdale), who gave me very helpful feedback. And last but not least, I thank Charlie Yost for proofreading the manuscript during one of his busier summers. This is the third book he has helped me edit. A mere thank you doesn't cut it. All of the people mentioned above are true friends who have graciously given of their time to make this project successful.

For my children, I wrote *Trains to Treblinka* to help keep the memory of Treblinka alive for your generation. Live your lives. Live your lives well. It has been over seventy-five years since the revolt. Now all who escaped and lived to tell their story are no longer with us, and many of the biographers who interviewed the survivors are deceased. All we have left are their stories—and we need them. It is important to study the past to learn these two lessons: the extent of what humans are capable of doing to each other, and the extent the inner spirit of man can accomplish in response to crisis. And that's the Treblinka elegy, a crisis of humanity. Learn both lessons. Love all people. And remember that in order to fully love, you must fully forgive.

CPSIA information can be obtained
at www.ICGtesting.com
Printed in the USA
BVHW030717280321
603577BV00024B/9